TWIN POWER
THE LOST CUP

EMMA LARKIN is the author of the first Twin Power adventure about Aoife and Aidan Power, *Twin Power: Throw In!* She is also the author of the 'Izzy's Magical Adventures in Sport' series. She is originally from Cork, but now lives in Kerry with her husband and four children.

TWIN POWER
THE LOST CUP

EMMA LARKIN

GAA, HISTORY and a MYSTERY

THE O'BRIEN PRESS
DUBLIN

First published 2023 by
The O'Brien Press Ltd,
12 Terenure Road East, Rathgar,
Dublin 6, D06 HD27
Ireland
Tel: +353 1 4923333; Fax: +353 1 4922777
E-mail: books@obrien.ie
Website: obrien.ie
The O'Brien Press is a member of Publishing Ireland.

ISBN: 978-1-78849-410-6

8 7 6 5 4 3 2 1
26 25 24 23

Printed and bound by Norhaven Paperback A/S, Denmark.

DEDICATION

For all the young readers and sports stars.
Keep reading, keep dreaming, keep playing!

ACKNOWLEDGEMENTS

A huge thank you to all the team at The O'Brien Press for their support and encouragement of the *Twin Power* series, especially my editor Helen Carr and designer Emma Byrne. Thanks to Lauren O'Neill for a second stunning cover; Lauren's artwork has vividly brought the *Twin Power* books to life. Thanks to Julianne McKeigue and all the team at the GAA Museum in Croke Park, for being so supportive of my books and for providing invaluable research assistance for *The Lost Cup*. I thoroughly enjoyed my tour of Croke Park and the GAA Museum! Thanks to Joe Harrington of the Lyreacrompane Heritage Group for his help in researching this book and for the interesting chat. Joe's extensive historical knowledge of our area in north Kerry was very helpful. Thank you to Chris Rychter for help with the Polish terms in the book. Thank you to my husband Robbie for reading the football-focused chapters with his expert eyes. His knowledge of Gaelic football, from years spent both on the pitch and side-line is crucial for me in ensuring accuracy in my books. Finally, thank you to my four children. I simply couldn't write my books without their help, support and encouragement.

CHAPTER 1

Aidan leaned casually against the fence surrounding his favourite place in the world, the pitch at Droichead Beag GAA club. It was a pleasant April evening. He was tired, but nicely so. He had just finished a tough but fun training session with his team, the Droichead Beag under-12 Gaelic football team. Now he was waiting for his dad, who was a coach with the team.

Aidan was by himself, which was unusual for him. His twin sister Aoife or his best friend Billy were usually by his side. Tonight, however, Aoife had a match with her girls' under-12 football team with the newly formed ladies' football club, Droichead/ Gorman. Aoife still trained and played matches with

Droichead GAA, but tonight a match for the ladies' club and training for Droichead had clashed and the match took precedence. Aidan wondered how they had got on and wished his dad would hurry up so that he could find out if their mam had texted the result.

Aidan's dad and the other under-12 coaches, Donie and Kathleen, were talking to Billy over at the other side of the pitch. *What's taking so long?* Aidan wondered. He hoped Billy wasn't in trouble. Billy could be a bit intense and hot-headed sometimes on the field of play. Aidan couldn't remember anything of note happening in the practice match this evening. Maybe they were just talking tactics about their match on Sunday. It was a winner-takes-all clash against their arch-rivals, Gorman, in the Division 1 under-12 county league final. But Aidan didn't think they would talk tactics to Billy without the rest of the team present.

Aidan kicked a bit of dirt next to him and re-adjusted his gear bag on his shoulder. The sun was warm, and it reminded Aidan of the beautiful day a year ago when his school football team had defeated their rival school, Gorman, in the final of the Star

Schools Cup. It was a lovely memory and always brought a smile to Aidan's face when he thought about it. The rest of the year had been good, too. Aoife had come back training with Droichead Beag GAA and the team had gone on to have a great season. Aoife, Aidan and Billy had become a well-oiled machine in the midfield/centre forward area, grounding the team and pushing them on to lots of victories, including the Division 2 under-12 county league. It had all gone so well. Everyone was really enjoying themselves and enjoying their football. Also, because they had won Division 2, they had been promoted to Division 1 for this year, which was a great achievement.

Aidan considered his group of friends on the team: John had gone from strength to strength in goals and his reflexes and shot stopping were improving all the time. Tina was relishing her role in the backs and Sara was turning into a really nippy forward who just seemed to know where to be to win the ball. All was good with the six of them in the gang. But that was then, and this was now. Things were a bit different now.

'OK, Aidan, let's head for home.'

Aidan looked up to see his dad walking quickly towards him.

'Where's Billy?' Aidan asked.

They usually all walked home together. Out of the corner of his eye, he saw the red and black of Billy's jersey disappear around the corner of the clubhouse. Billy had gone home ahead of them. *That's weird,* Aidan thought.

'Is Billy OK, Dad?' Aidan asked.

'Oh, I'd say he's fine,' his dad replied quickly.

'It's just strange that he didn't wait for me,' Aidan persisted.

'Maybe he had to get home in a hurry for something,' his dad replied.

Aidan wasn't convinced.

'What were you, Donie and Kathleen talking to him about?' he asked. 'Is he in trouble?'

'No, he's not in trouble,' his dad sighed. 'Look, Aidan, I'm sure Billy will tell you himself when he's ready. Come on, race you home.'

Dad took off sprinting. Aidan was caught off guard, but quickly righted himself and tore off after his father. His heart wasn't in it, though.

* * *

Despite his reluctance, Aidan, with his powerful running stride, had almost caught up with his father
as they reached the entrance to Amber Fields, the
small estate where the Powers lived. Amber Fields
contained just four houses in a horseshoe shape and
was only two hundred metres from the entrance to
the Droichead Beag GAA pitch. Next to the pitch,
was the Droichead Beag primary school. Aoife and
Aidan loved living in such close proximity to the
pitch, but not to the school, as they had no excuse
for being late!

Aidan and his dad slowed down and walked up
to the front door of number 2. They turned their
heads to the sound of a car rumbling in the entrance
of Amber Fields. It was Aoife, Mam and Clare – the
youngest Power sibling – coming home from Aoife's
match.

'Did you win?' Aidan greeted his twin sister with
a question.

'Not even a "Hi, Mam, how are you?"' their mam laughed.

Aidan's bluntness didn't bother Aoife; she'd have asked the exact same question if the roles had been reversed.

'Yup,' she grinned, 'close match, we just won by two points in the end. Bally had some talented players.'

'Did you score?' Aidan continued.

'Yeah, a goal and two points,' Aoife replied. 'We won by 2-10 to 2-8. Sara scored a lot of the points. She was playing corner forward, she's flying it. Maeve scored two points as well I think.'

'Was Tina there?' Aidan asked.

'No,' Aoife replied sadly.

'Aoife, Aidan, give me a hand with the shopping please,' said their mam, interrupting their catch-up.

'How was training?' Aoife asked Aidan as she hauled a bag of potatoes out of the boot.

'Oh, grand,' Aidan replied. 'It was weird though,' he continued. 'Dad, Donie and Kathleen were talking to Billy for ages at the end of training, and then he took off home without saying anything to me.'

'That *is* weird,' Aoife agreed. 'Did he get in trouble at training?'

'No,' Aidan replied. 'Sure, he hasn't gotten in trouble in ages, he's playing really well too.'

Billy could be a bit moody and didn't always cope well with what he thought of as unfair decisions in matches. He tended to lose his temper when he got frustrated on the pitch. But Aidan was correct, Aoife thought. He'd been in great form recently.

'Maybe he felt sick or something?' she speculated. 'Why don't we call over to him in a while?'

'Yeah, maybe,' Aidan was noncommittal.

Billy was a good friend of both Aoife and Aidan, and he lived right next door to them in number 1 Amber Fields.

'Aoife, Aidan, come on, let's get that shopping in!'

Mam's voice sounded from inside the house and Aoife and Aidan moved quickly to get the rest of the bags out of the boot.

CHAPTER 2

The following morning Aoife and Aidan, late as usual, hurried along the path towards Droichead Beag school. They – along with their friends, John, Billy, Tina and Sara – were in sixth class and were looking forward to the Easter holidays, which were only a week away.

'Strange that Billy didn't walk to school with us this morning,' Aidan noted.

Aoife turned to her brother.

'This carry-on with Billy is bothering you, Aidan, isn't it?' she asked carefully.

'I just hope I didn't do anything to annoy him,' Aidan replied. 'It was really weird that he left training last night without talking to me, and he wasn't playing FIFA online last night either.'

'Hmm,' Aoife said. 'He can be moody, Aidan. Maybe he had a fight with his brother? I don't think you did anything; sure, you are great friends.'

'Did he say anything to you?' Aidan asked. He knew that Aoife and Billy were close.

'No,' Aoife replied. 'I'd have told you anyway, you know that.'

The twins were fiercely loyal to each other. As they arrived at the school gates, Aidan noticed Billy ahead of them walking quickly towards the door of the school. Again, Aidan thought how odd it was that he hadn't walked to school with them.

'What's up, Twin Power?' John shouted loudly, interrupting Aidan's thoughts.

John slammed the door of his mother's car closed with a flourish, adding, 'See you, Mam,' almost as an afterthought.

Mrs Tracey waved at the twins and gave them a big smile as she drove away.

'Hi, John,' Aoife laughed. 'Twin Power are in flying form, aren't we, Aidan?'

'Yup, we are,' Aidan gave a small smile.

He's still worried about Billy, Aoife thought.

'All set for the big match against Gorman on Sunday?' John continued. 'I'm going to keep a clean sheet,' he grinned, rubbing his hands together. 'These magic hands are going to save all the goals.

'I believe you, John,' Aoife laughed.

Aidan just smiled. He couldn't shake the small niggle of worry in the pit of his stomach about this match. It just felt like it had come on them very quickly and that they weren't ready. *Maybe I'm being silly,* he thought, shaking his head.

'Hi, gang,' Tina waved at them as they walked in the school gates, Sara by her side.

'You *just* about made it before the bell,' Sara grinned.

'That was your fault, wasn't it, Aidan?' Aoife said with a wink, trying to cheer up her brother.

Aidan gave a half-hearted smile. Everyone in the Amber Fields gang knew that when the twins were late, it was nearly always Aoife's fault.

'So, what exciting topic will Ms Casey be teaching us about today in history?' John asked, making a bored face.

Ms Casey was the sixth-class teacher in Droichead Beag and was not a favourite of the Amber Fields gang.

'Probably something boring from the Stone Age,' Sara groaned.

'Yeah, I am getting a bit sick of learning about really old stones and stuff,' Tina said. 'But I suppose she has to follow the syllabus.' Tina was calm and rational about everything.

'I wish we still had Ms Kelly teaching us,' Aoife added wistfully.

Ms Kelly had taught the gang the previous year. She was teaching the current fifth class now. She was a great footballer and a former county All-Star player. She was also the school's football coach and did a lot of P.E. with the class.

'Me too,' Sara said. 'Ms Casey only takes us out to do P.E. when she absolutely *has* to.'

Sara was really enjoying playing football with Droichead Beag GAA club and Droichead/Gorman ladies' football club and was turning into a great corner forward, a natural point-scorer. She had unbelievable accuracy in her kicks. She would have loved to play more football, or any other sport, in school.

'Some hope of that,' John groaned. 'Why doesn't she follow the curriculum with P.E. eh, Tina?' he added.

'Why are you asking me?' Tina replied, suddenly defensive.

'Well, you usually want everything to be done right,' John retorted. 'Also, you aren't playing a lot of sport at the moment, so I suppose I was just wondering what's going on?'

Oh no! Aidan thought. The gang had all noticed that Tina wasn't playing as much football as she used to, but no one had really made a big deal of it, not wanting to upset her. But John, with his typical bluntness, had brought the issue out in the open.

Maybe it's no harm, Aidan thought, *get her to talk about it, sort things out. That really helped Aoife last year.*

'C'mon guys, we're going to get in trouble with Ms Casey for being late,' Aoife said quickly, seeing the look of dismay on Tina's face and hoping to defuse the situation.

At that same moment, Ms Casey popped her head out the door of the school and beckoned furiously for the children to hurry up and come into the class-room. Tina's reluctance to play football was forgot-ten, for now anyway.

The children filed into the classroom. 'Hi, Aidan, hi, Aoife,' Billy grinned, as the twins took their places next to him in the classroom. The desks in sixth class were set up in long parallel rows. Aidan sat just to the left of Billy and Aoife to the right.

All seems good here, Aoife thought happily.

'Hi, Billy,' Aidan replied with a smile. *Maybe I was imagining things,* he thought.

'Quiet,' Ms Casey called out loudly. 'Time to get some work done. Before we start today, I have some good news for you about your school tour.'

A murmur of excitement ran through the room.

'This year,' Ms Casey continued, 'fifth and sixth class are going on a very exciting school trip to Dublin next month.'

'Are we going to the zoo?' John shouted out excit-edly.

'No, John,' Ms Casey replied sternly. '*Lámha suas,* hands up, John, if you want to ask a question. We are going somewhere that I'm sure you will all really enjoy. Ms Kelly has organised a great tour for us: we are going on a trip to Croke Park and the GAA Museum which is—'

Ms Casey wasn't even able to finish her sentence as the classroom became a cauldron of noise, the children whooping and hollering with delight! Billy turned to Aidan, a huge smile on his face.

'This is going to be class, Aidan.'

'I know, I can't believe it,' Aidan replied with a grin, equally happy with the announcement about the school tour, and the fact that Billy was chatting to him normally. He must have definitely imagined any weirdness between them. Maybe Dad and the other coaches were just giving him some tips about football in general yesterday evening when they were talking to him.

'*Ciúnas*,' Ms Casey raised her voice. 'Let me finish what I was going to say. We are going to visit Croke Park, we will be getting a tour of the stadium and then we will also visit the GAA Museum, which is part of the stadium.

'So, in advance of our trip, I think that we are going to focus on some modern history and in particular, the history of the GAA, building on what your learned with Ms Kelly last year. We will focus on the history of the GAA around the time of the War of Independence, since the centenary of that was so recent. This will help us to get the full benefit of our trip to the GAA Museum. Sound like a plan?'

'I like this plan, *a mhúinteoir*,' Tina said brightly.

No more history about old stones, Aoife thought happily.

'Maybe we could find out about the Lost Cup of Droichead Beag?' Aidan said quietly.

'The lost what?' Billy and Aoife asked together.

'What did you say Aidan? What's the Lost Cup?' Ms Casey asked (she had supersonic hearing). 'This sounds interesting.'

'Well, I'm not really sure,' Aidan continued, shy now in talking about it. 'Apparently, it's some county GAA cup that was won by Coyle Gaels back in the 1920s or something. I heard Nana and Grandad Power mention it once. They didn't tell me very much about it, though.'

'Remind me again, Aidan, what is Coyle Gaels?' Ms Casey asked.

Ms Casey was from a different county and wasn't always familiar with local GAA teams.

'Coyle Gaels is a divisional team, *a mhúinteoir*,' Aidan answered. 'It's made up of Droichead Beag, Gorman and Carrick. The best players from the three clubs play together in some of the county GAA competitions, the divisional ones.'

'It's named after the River Coyle, which runs through Carrick and all the way to Droichead, is that right?' Ms Casey asked.

'Yes, *a mhúinteor*,' Aidan confirmed.

'So, this Lost Cup, it's never been found, I imagine, is that the story?'

'Yes,' Aidan said, warming to his subject matter now. 'But I'm not sure if it's a sort of local legend or if it's actually true. I mean, I'd like to think it is true. They say that it was a really big cup, not as big as the Sam Maguire, but not far off, and it just vanished!'

'I mean, it *must* be hidden somewhere nearby if it's called the Lost Cup of Droichead Beag,' John said suddenly. 'This is so cool, a treasure buried in Droichead!'

'It certainly is, John,' Ms Casey replied beaming.

'Well, Aidan,' she continued. 'That's very interesting. Who knows, you might be able to find out more about the Lost Cup at the Croke Park museum. You might even solve the mystery for us.'

Aidan grinned happily. Football, history and a mystery to solve – things were looking up.

CHAPTER 3

The gang tumbled out of the classroom at 3pm on the dot. They didn't want to waste any more time indoors when the sun was shining. Aidan had been staring out at the blue sky all day and thinking how he could be kicking a ball or cycling his bike along the new greenway. Anything except sitting in a hot classroom, trying to understand how to work out the profit in a maths problem. Aidan didn't enjoy maths at all.

'Right, match on the green in half an hour?' he asked, throwing his bag over his shoulder.

'I wish! John replied as they walked down the front steps of the school. 'I have to go home; my dad is collecting me today.'

'Why aren't you coming to our house?' Aoife asked.

John was the only member of the gang who didn't live in Amber Fields. He lived on a farm about three kilometres outside Droichead Beag. Most days, he went to Aoife and Aidan's house after school. Mr Power looked after John until his mam finished work in the local secondary school and picked him up on the way home.

John sighed deeply, pushing his dark hair that just couldn't be tamed out of his eyes. 'Calving is still happening. You townie folks wouldn't know much about that,' he added lightheartedly.

John was the joker of the group. It was a constant source of annoyance to him that he lived outside the town and away from the rest of the gang. They all reckoned that John secretly enjoyed life on the farm, he just didn't want to admit it.

'Excuse me,' Aoife replied. 'Our Nana and Grandad Power still have some cattle; we help out on their farm sometimes.'

'Not much, Aoife, to be fair,' Aidan laughed.

'Calving seems to be going on forever this year

John,' Billy commented.

'Don't talk to me, Billy,' John replied good-naturedly. 'It's never-ending. We're almost there now, Dad says, but he's busy today, there's a cow sick as well, so I need to go home and help with other stuff on the farm. Right, see you tomorrow so,' he waved as they heard a beep from John's dad's battered farm jeep.

'I can't play either,' Sara said as the remaining five of the gang walked towards Amber Fields. 'I'm going to the airport with my mam and dad to collect Dzia-dek Staś– my grandad.

'Oh, is he visiting from Poland?' Aoife asked excitedly.

'Yes,' Sara grinned. 'I can't wait to see him. I haven't seen him since last summer. He retired from work earlier this year and Mam says he is bored. So, he is coming on a long visit to see us.'

'Has he ever been in Ireland before?' Tina asked.

'No, never,' Sara replied. 'We've been living here since I was four, but he has always been so busy with work, his soccer teams – or football as he calls it – so he never had time to visit. Also, we go back every summer, so he sees us then.'

'Does he work with soccer teams?' Billy asked.

'Oh yes, he's a coach, that was his job. He LOVED it!' Sara replied. 'He used to play for the Polish soccer team when he was younger. He was very good, my dad says. He has been coaching professional teams in Poland for years –since he stopped playing. He has loads of UEFA coaching badges and stuff.'

'Wow,' Aidan commented. 'Does your mam think he is bored because he's stopped coaching?'

'Yes,' Sara replied. They think he should have kept going, he is still really fit. But he told my dad that he has a new challenge starting in the autumn, whatever that means.'

'What position did he play for Poland?' Aoife asked.

'He was a striker,' Sara replied, smiling.

'Well, that should have been obvious,' Tina laughed.

'Yeah, now we know why you are such a good forward in football,' Billy grinned.

'Is he on FIFA? Aidan asked. 'He might be one of the "icon" players on it?'

'I don't know about that,' Sara said. 'His name is Stanisław Novak.'

'We'll check out his rating this evening,' Aidan laughed.

'Right, well, I've got to run,' Sara said. 'Mam and Dad will be waiting for me to go the airport.'

Sara ran off into number 4 Amber Fields, which was at the front left-hand side of the horseshoe shape that made up the four houses in Amber Fields. The school was in such proximity to Amber Fields that the gang had arrived home without even realising it, engrossed as they were in the story of Stanisław Novak, Sara's grandad.

'So, it's just the four of us,' Aidan said to Aoife, Billy and Tina. 'See you shortly.'

'Erm, I won't make it either,' Tina shifted uncomfortably, as she chewed on the end of her long blonde plait and moved from one foot to the other. 'I have to take Max for a walk.'

Max was Tina's gorgeous dog. He was a golden retriever and was so lovely and friendly. He loved the company of the gang.

'Sure, why don't you bring him with you?' Aoife

asked gently. 'We can kick around for a bit and then take Max for a walk together afterwards?'

'No, he would be restless watching us play football,' Tina said quickly.

'He often watches us play,' Billy began, but Aoife nudged him in the ribs. 'Hey, what did you do that for?' he looked at Aoife crossly, rubbing his side.

'I have to go,' Tina said quickly. 'Mam said to make sure to take him for a walk after school.'

With that, she was gone, into number 3. Tina's house was at the back left-hand side of the horse-shoe shape, between the Novaks and the Powers.

'Seriously, that hurt,' Billy started after Tina had run indoors.

'No, it didn't,' Aoife dismissed him quickly. 'I just wanted you to leave her alone.'

'I wasn't saying anything bad,' Billy protested.

'I know,' Aoife said. 'But she doesn't seem to want to play football right now and I don't want to upset her any more. Especially after John's comment earlier at school.'

'John was only saying what we are all thinking, Aoife,' Aidan joined in. 'He thinks she might be better off talking about whatever is bothering her, like you did last year – eventually.'

'That was different,' Aoife said slowly, thinking back to when she told her friends about how Tommy Doyle from Gorman had bullied her and the horrible effect it had on her. She still shuddered thinking about that time. She had missed playing football so much and her life was so much better now that she had stood up to Tommy. Now she had *two* football teams to play for. Her life felt good right now, lots of football and good friends.

'I don't think anything happened to Tina the way it did to me,' Aoife said. 'I think she has just lost interest in football right now. Haven't you noticed that she makes excuses not to play matches in the green? She says that she has to help with dinner or bring Max for a walk. In school, she doesn't play soccer or basketball at break, she plays chase or just chats to some of the girls. She doesn't talk about sport much; I think she still wants to play football, because she still asks me about matches, but I'm not sure. I think if we keep pestering her, it will make things worse.'

'I don't know,' Aidan said shaking his head. 'That

all sounds a bit complicated to me, Aoife. She always enjoyed football. Why are we tip-toeing around this, why can't we just ask her?'

Aidan was very practical and liked solving problems and getting things done.

'What do you think, Billy?' he asked his friend, who Aidan suddenly realised had gone quiet.

'Erm, I don't know really,' Billy muttered. 'Aoife might be right. Sometimes people don't like talking about things until they are ready.'

Hmm, Aoife thought, *this has all gotten a bit deep. I need to change the subject here.*

She wondered if Billy was still talking about Tina or was it more about himself now. He was another person who didn't like to talk about problems.

'Will the three of us cycle down to the new greenway?' Aoife asked loudly. 'I want to take some photos down there for my art. We could bring a ball and kick around in the clearing part, near the new picnic tables.'

'Sounds like a plan,' Aidan said quickly.

'OK,' Billy nodded. 'Give me a few minutes and we'll head off.'

CHAPTER 4

Half an hour later, Aoife, Aidan and Billy hopped on their bikes, and headed past Droichead Beag GAA pitch, past their school and towards the centre of Droichead Beag village. This didn't take long as Droichead, as it was known for short, was a very small village. Apart from the school and the GAA pitch, it just had a shop, a pub, a post office, a café, an art gallery and then the petrol station on the way out of the village, as you headed for Gorman and then on to Carrick, the big town. Gorman was even smaller than Droichead. It was more of a townland; it just had one small shop next to its GAA pitch in its so-called centre. What it did have was a huge area around it where there were lots of farms and rural houses, so they had plenty of players for their GAA club.

Gorman bordered Droichead Beag and the rivalry between the two neighbouring clubs was as old as the GAA itself. Droichead had a smaller population, so in theory, it should have struggled against Gorman. But Droichead had a history of having skilful players, with these skills being passed down through the generations. Aoife and Aidan's family, the Powers, were once such family. Billy's family, the Donovans, were another. Complementing this was the arrival of families to Droichead from other counties such as Tina's family, the O'Sheas, or even from other countries such as Sara's family, the Novaks, who had moved to Ireland from Poland. Families were drawn to Droichead as the price of houses in the big cities was getting very high and Droichead was a lovely place to live, with great broadband so people were able to work from home, like Mr Power did.

The combination of new and old families and a great coaching atmosphere in Droichead Beag GAA club was really paying off and the club was doing very well at all levels.

Aoife, Aidan and Billy were heading for the bridge that gave Droichead its name. 'Droichead Beag' was Irish and literally translated to 'small bridge' in English. The bridge was a focal point in the village. It was made of old stone and was well maintained. Colourful flower boxes adorned it in the summer.

Below the bridge, down by the River Coyle, was a river walk. This walk was being extended into a path that locals called the greenway. There had always been a river walk, but the bridge in Droichead Beag had been the finishing point of the walk. It started in Carrick and went along the path of the River Coyle, through Gorman and finished in Droichead Beag by the river. It was popular with walkers and cyclists. There was a lovely picnic table area under the bridge in Droichead.

This new extended greenway continued in the opposite direction to Gorman. It looped away from the river, following an old path that headed in the direction of the Power twins' grandparents' farm, and continued towards John's farm and toward the ruins of an old forge. The county council were doing lots of work on it. It was supposed to be ready for the summer tourist season.

Aoife, Aidan and Billy parked up their bikes under the bridge and waved at Kathleen who was working on the flower boxes, getting them ready for the summer. Kathleen was one of the under-12 coaches with Droichead, along with the twins' dad. She also owned the café near the bridge.

'Well, how are my star footballers?' Kathleen beamed as she poured more compost into the flower boxes.

'We're good,' the trio chimed.

'Where are the rest of your partners in crime today?' Kathleen asked.

'They're all busy,' Aoife replied. 'Calving and what not.'

'Ah yes, John is a busy man this time of year,' Kathleen nodded. 'I see you managed to bring a ball with you on the bike, Billy,' she laughed. 'I wouldn't doubt you. Practising for the competition all the time, no doubt,' she continued. 'I'd say the ball doesn't leave your hand. A true Donovan.'

Aoife and Aidan looked at Billy curiously as he dismounted his bike looking uncomfortable.

'What competition?' they whispered at him furiously.

'I dunno,' Billy muttered. 'She's confused, I'd say.'

'See you later, Kathleen,' he waved. 'C'mon, let's go,' he said quickly.

Kathleen looked surprised at the abrupt end to the conversation, but returned to her flower boxes. 'See you all on Sunday for the big match,' she shouted after them.

'So, what's the story with this greenway path?' Billy asked quickly as the trio headed off in the direction of the Power farm.

'I think it's an old path that used to lead along to a forge and some other buildings, but they're in ruins now. Maybe it was another old village, I'm not sure.' Aoife replied. 'It goes along the back of our grandparents' farm and then further on it passes John's farm. It's about three kilometres long, I think,' she added. 'There's an old kiln near our grandparents' farm that they are doing up as well. I want to take some photos of the kiln and the old ruins with my phone so that I can draw them.'

Aoife was an exceptionally talented artist. After

football, it was her next favourite thing to do.

'There is a bit of a clearing near the kiln,' she added. 'The council are putting more picnic tables and stuff there. We can kick around there for a while.'

Billy nodded. 'Sounds like a plan,' he said. 'Maybe we can call into your grandparents for some cake too,' he grinned.

Aoife laughed. 'You read my mind, Billy.'

Aidan was walking quietly, listening to Billy and Aoife chatting good-naturedly. Now Billy was asking Aoife what a kiln was. She wasn't sure, but was going to ask their grandparents.

Something was niggling at Aidan. Billy was never this interested in Aoife's art or local history, or anything except football usually. *What competition had Kathleen being talking about?* Aidan wondered again. He was reminded of something that Darragh had said a few weeks ago. Darragh was their friend from Gorman. He had started out as their enemy, because of his allegiance to Tommy Doyle, but that had all changed after the Star Schools final last year and now Darragh often dropped over to Droichead with Maeve, another Gorman player, to kick ball or just hang out. Darragh had said something to Aidan about how Billy thought that Aidan was always the best at football skills. Aidan hadn't been quite sure what Darragh was talking about at the time and had changed the subject, embarrassed at talking about 'who was the best at things', but now it was all coming back to him.

Aidan was suddenly aware that the conversation had changed between Aoife and Billy, Aoife had said something about competition and Billy had gone very quiet. *Ah ha, now it makes sense,* Aidan thought. Billy had been chattering on to Aoife about anything and everything except football, ever since Kathleen has asked him about the competition. He must have been hoping that the twins would forget about it. What *was* this mystery competition?

'Ah c'mon Billy, you can tell us, you tell us everything. What's this competition about?' Aidan asked.

'Oh, all right,' Billy sighed. 'It's stupid really. I don't know why I didn't just tell the two of you.'

Aoife looked puzzled.

'Just spill, Billy,' she said quickly.

'Do you remember a few weeks ago at under-12

training, we did a skills competition?'

'Yeah, I remember,' Aidan said.

'We were doing the pick-up, punt kick skill. Some zig-zag solos and the like,' Aoife added.

'Yeah, that one,' Billy confirmed.

'You won it,' Aidan said.

'Yeah,' Billy sighed again.

'Just about!' Aoife laughed.

'We tied for second, Aoife, didn't we?' Aidan asked.

'You did,' Billy replied. 'You were both literally just one point off my score.'

'So, what's the problem?' Aoife asked.

'Well, it turns out that the winner gets to go onto a regional skills competition.'

'So that's you?' Aidan asked.

'Yes,' Billy said again.

'That great! Wait, why are you not happy?' Aidan asked incredulously.

'Yeah, am I missing something here?' Aoife asked. 'That's brilliant news, why didn't you tell us?'

Billy kicked at a piece of dirt on the track. They had reached a part of the greenway that didn't have tarmac as yet and it was rough underfoot.

'I just felt like I shouldn't have won,' Billy spluttered. 'I mean we were just messing around that night; we weren't taking it seriously. One of you would be just as good as me. I'd prefer if we were all going.'

'Wait, is that what our dad and Donie and Kathleen were talking to you about at the end of training the other night?' Aidan asked, realisation dawning on him.

'Yeah,' Billy replied. 'Sorry I went home without you. I just felt weird about it all.'

'Look, I get it, Billy. Well actually I don't really,' Aidan said. 'This is great news; sure, we are happy for you.'

'Do you feel better about it now?' Aoife asked.

'Em, I'm a bit excited about it now,' Billy replied. 'Darragh won it in Gorman and there is going to be training before the regional competition so it will be good to have him there as well.'

'Oh,' Aidan said quietly. 'When did he tell you that?'

'The other night, when we were playing FIFA online,' Billy replied vaguely. 'I don't think you were playing that night.'

I definitely wasn't! Aidan thought, a wave of annoyance sweeping over him.

'That's great that you'll know someone there,' Aoife said brightly, but her voice faded as she saw the look on Aidan's face.

'Look, we're at the clearing,' she said, changing the subject. 'Let's kick ball for a while.'

The three of them kicked around for half an hour but it was subdued, none of the usual messing. When they were done, they walked quietly – too quietly – back to their bikes.

'What's up with you?' Aoife asked Aidan when Billy was out of earshot on his bike, slightly ahead of the twins.

'Nothing, I'm just tired,' Aidan replied quickly and took off on his bike across the bridge, heading for Amber Fields.

Aoife felt a strange feeling of foreboding as she watched her brother pedalling furiously ahead of her.

CHAPTER 5

Sunday came around very quickly. Aoife and Aidan had got up early, eaten their porridge, and now they were kicking a ball around in the back garden.

Today was the day that their team, the Droichead Beag under 12s were playing Gorman in a winner-takes-all clash in Division 1 of the county league. Both teams were unbeaten in the league, which had started in March; today was the last match. It was Droichead's first time ever playing in Division 1, the highest division in the county. To be unbeaten so far in their first season in Division 1 was a great achievement, whatever the result today. However, now that it had come down to this, a must-win game against

Gorman, they wanted to win outright more than anything.

'I'm a bit nervous about the match,' Aidan admitted to his twin.

'Yeah, me too,' Aoife replied. 'Gorman have been very quiet. Even Darragh and Maeve, who are sound, haven't been saying much about it. I think they are quietly confident.'

'Hmm. Yeah, Darragh is playing well this year,' Aidan said.

Aidan felt annoyed at Darragh for a reason that he just couldn't quite put his finger on. The whole thing about the skills competition and Billy playing FIFA online with Darragh without him was just weird. But he had to admit, even if he didn't really like the fact, that Darragh was flying it at football this year.

'Since Maeve's mam and that other guy, Barry, started helping coach the team, they all seem to be playing a lot better.'

'Annie Doyle has really calmed down, too,' Aoife said. 'Maeve was telling me. She said she even laughs sometimes at training now.'

'I'd have to see that before I'd believe it,' Aidan smiled.

'Why do you feel nervous?' Aoife asked.

'I don't know,' Aidan replied. 'I have this weird feeling about it. Last year, we were all playing really well together, but this year, I just feel that it hasn't clicked. I know we've won all our games, but something isn't right. I mean, Tina has missed most matches. We'll really need her in the backs today because Maeve is on fire for Gorman apparently. She scored 1-7 against Bally. And Billy is in funny form. I think he's a bit distracted by this skills competition.'

'Ah, I don't think he is,' Aoife defended Billy quickly. She was worried that Aidan was being a bit unfair to Billy about the skills competition. She had seen how his face dropped when he realised that Billy and Darragh had been playing FIFA without him. Billy was like a brother to Aoife and Aidan. They lived next door to each other and had grown up together. Aoife felt that Aidan was struggling a bit with new friends coming into their group.

'Well, why are *you* nervous?' Aidan put it back on Aoife. 'Are you still worried about facing Tommy

Doyle? I thought that was all sorted.'

'No, it's not him,' Aoife said. 'Well, it is, and it isn't. I'm not nervous about playing him after what he did to me when we were younger. I am totally over that, thanks to all the help I got from our gang last year. No, I'm nervous about him because he has been so quiet. So has Ellie. No bragging, no trash talk. That worries me.'

'Yeah, I know what you mean,' Aidan nodded.

'But we need to be positive,' Aoife said loudly. 'You are always the sensible one telling me that,' she accused Aidan.

'You're right,' Aidan grinned. 'Didn't we win the Star Schools Cup against all the odds. We can do this.'

The sound of a dog barking distracted the twins and they both turned in the direction of the O' Sheas' house next door, Tina's house.

'That must be Max,' Aoife said.

Aoife and Aidan quickly climbed up the branches of the strong oak tree at the end of their garden and into the tree house that their mam and dad had built halfway up it. It was one of the twins' favourite places to hang out. It was a great place to come and read a book, play a game of cards – or draw a picture in Aoife's case. It also had lovely views of the surrounding countryside, including the gardens of their neighbours, the O'Shea's where Tina lived and the Donovan's on the other side, Billy's house.

'Yup, that's Max barking,' Aidan confirmed.

'He's happy-barking,' Aoife laughed. 'He's playing with Pádraig.'

'Pádraig!' Aidan shouted over to Tina's younger brother. 'How's things?'

Pádraig turned his head to see where the voices were coming from.

'Oh, hi, Aidan, hi, Aoife!' he waved enthusiastically. 'Nearly time for the match. I'm just playing with Max to tire him out before we go. I can't wait to see you all beat those Gorman idiots.'

'Erm, right,' Aoife replied. 'We'll see. Is Tina around?'

'Yeah, she's inside.' Pádraig continued. 'She said she can't play 'cos her boots are too small, but I reckon she's lying. I think she doesn't like playing football with boys anymore. I heard her talking to Mam about it.'

Aoife and Aidan exchanged looks.

'Which is stupid,' Pádraig was still talking. 'Because she's taller than nearly all of the boys and she's really strong.'

'Yeah, she's a brilliant corner back,' Aidan agreed.

'I know, right?' Pádraig replied. 'I heard her saying that it was embarrassing playing with boys. Mam tried to change her mind, but no joy. Girls! I just don't get them sometimes. No offence, Aoife.'

'None taken,' Aoife replied. 'Look we'd better go, its nearly time to leave.'

She suddenly felt uncomfortable with Pádraig revealing Tina's private conversations with her mother.

'That's a fairly common thing for girls in my secondary school to say to me,' Aoife's mam said to her as they got out of their car and walked towards the big pitch in Carrick where the under-12 league final match against Gorman was about to take place.

Aidan, Clare and Mr Power were walking ahead.

Mr Power had a bag of footballs dangling over his shoulder and Clare was kicking a ball along the path. Aidan was quiet.

'But *why* is it embarrassing?' Aoife asked her mother, having told her in confidence what Pádraig had said. 'I don't get it. It's just the same as playing with girls.'

'Some people think that, Aoife,' her mam replied. 'But some girls, particularly when they hit their teenage years, start feeling more self-conscious around boys and a bit awkward. The same can be true for boys. For girls, sometimes they are worried about the boys getting bigger and taller, that the girls might get hurt. Some girls are nervous about getting sweaty and messy around boys, or they could be afraid that people will laugh if they get something wrong. Also, some girls in my school would say to me that they don't always like wearing the football gear as they start getting older and taller.'

'But Tina has played football with boys all her life,' Aoife continued. 'I just don't get why it would feel weird for her now.'

'Maybe try and talk to her about it, gently,' her

mam encouraged. 'Tell her that because she is getting taller, that she is also getting stronger and that her body can do fantastic skilful things on the football pitch. Tell her to look at all the different shapes and sizes of people that you see on sports teams, boys and girls. Trust me when I say to you, Aoife, that everyone is more conscious of themselves, than looking at other people on the pitch and what they might get wrong. Remind Tina of the fun and friendship that you all have on the team. Here's my top tip: tell her that you can keep up football and sport *and* try out new things as well, it's not either or.'

'I will,' Aoife replied. 'Thanks, Mam. I wish I'd known this before today and I might have been able to convince her to play in the match.'

'Well, put that out of your head now and just concentrate on the game in hand,' Mrs Power said wisely.

'I will, Mam,' Aoife said confidently. 'Right, let's do this,' she said loudly, running towards Aidan and shouldering him lightly, before continuing through the big gates of Carrick GAA.

CHAPTER 6

Aidan and Aoife sat outside the changing rooms lacing up their boots. It was another unseasonably hot April afternoon, and they didn't want to go inside. Their dad was on the pitch with Donie and Kathleen, the other coaches, setting up some cones for a warm-up.

Billy sauntered through the gates, his dark hair glinting in the afternoon sunshine. Even though it was April, Billy's skin was tanned. The first hint of sunshine and he turned a golden colour. He was smiling and looked more relaxed than the last time the twins had seen him. Come to think of it, Aidan thought, they hadn't seen Billy since the day on the greenway, last Thursday. Today was Sunday. They usually saw Billy every day.

'We haven't seen Billy in a few days,' Aoife said out loud, seemingly reading Aidan's mind.

'I literally just had that thought,' Aidan replied.

'Twin jinx,' Aoife grinned. 'Maybe he was at skills practice for the competition,' she continued.

No sooner had the words left her mouth than Darragh came running in the gate, wearing the blue and white of Gorman. The twins watched as he caught up with Billy and the two boys walked towards them, talking animatedly.

'Hi, Aoife, hi, Aidan,' Darragh greeted them enthusiastically. 'How's things with you two?'

Darragh seemed to have gotten even taller since they'd last seen him. He was nearly as tall as Billy now. Darragh had wavy blond hair that he was letting grow; it was long enough now that he needed to tie it up for matches. That's what he was doing now, talking to them with a bobble in his mouth as he pulled his hair together at the back of his head.

'Not bad, Darragh,' Aoife replied. 'I can't wait for the summer holidays.'

'Same here,' Darragh replied. 'At least you have

that cool school tour to Croke Park before then,' he continued. 'Billy was telling me. I'm *so* jealous. We're going to some boring old place. Don't they realise that it's our last year in Gorman school? They should be pulling out all the stops for us!'

Aoife laughed. Darragh was good company. Making friends with Maeve and Darragh was one of the good things that had come out of the whole Tommy Doyle bullying situation last year.

'So what position are you playing today, Darragh?' Aidan asked.

'Midfield,' Darragh replied. 'I've been playing there for the past few matches. Annie used to play me as a centre back, but Maeve's mam and Barry tried me out in midfield, and it seems to be going well. I like playing there.'

'Billy or I will be marking you so,' Aidan smiled.

'Yeah, I dunno am I looking forward to that!' Darragh laughed. 'Where are you playing, Aoife?' he asked. 'I thought you used play midfield?'

'I still do sometimes,' Aoife replied. 'I generally do play in midfield for the girls' team. But they play me at centre forward here and I love it. Less marking, more scoring! Well, that's the plan anyway,' she finished with a grin.

'Gorman won't have Tommy marking you anyway, don't worry,' Darragh said seriously. 'He's playing full forward today. And Maeve is centre forward like you. I'd say it'll be Israel marking you. He's super-fast. Ah, but you'll be well able for him.'

'What team are you even going for, Darragh?' Billy laughed. 'You're like an honorary Droichead player at this stage!'

'Ah no way, boy,' Darragh replied jokingly. 'I'm Gorman through and through. You are all still sound though,' he laughed. 'I was nearly looking for a transfer last year. It was so bad with Annie coaching. But things are much better now, she has really calmed down.'

'What about Tommy?' Aidan asked seriously. 'Has he calmed down?'

'Ah you know Tommy,' Darragh said nervously.

'I don't really!' Aidan retorted.

An awkward silence followed.

'Oh look, here come John and Sara,' Billy said, relief in his voice at having changed the subject away from Tommy. There was a hint of tension between Aidan and Darragh, which was weird. They usually got on very well.

'I have brand new goalie gloves,' John shouted, waving shiny new red and black gloves.

'They are the Droichead colours,' Sara was nodding enthusiastically. 'Aren't they class?'

'They're so cool,' Aoife agreed.

The gang started chattering quickly and nervous excitement filled the air about the soon-to-start match. The usual pre-match nerves were evident and talking helped a lot of them. Darragh was in flying form, making everyone laugh. They were all engrossed in his funny story about a dog that ran onto the pitch at their county skills practice. Billy was adding bits to the story as it went along, and Aoife noticed two things. Firstly, how relaxed Billy was around Darragh and secondly, how quiet Aidan was. It didn't bode well.

'I love a dog on the pitch story,' Sara was saying gleefully.

No one noticed the strong and powerful shape of Gorman's Tommy Doyle entering the pitch, Ellie

Ryan beside him. Darragh's story was reaching its comedic climax, '... and then the dog started picking up all the cones and moving them, so we were kicking from the wrong place!' and everyone burst out laughing.

'That skills practice sounds like gas craic altogether,' Tommy's voice boomed.

He was grinning, but it was hard to tell if it was genuine or not. *Probably not,* Aoife thought. *Tommy is always so sarcastic.*

'Tommy, bud, I didn't see you come in there,' Darragh laughed. 'I was just telling the lads the dog story. Remember I was telling you about it yesterday, wasn't I? It was so funny.'

'Yeah, I tell you I'm sorry I didn't try harder to win that skills competition now,' Tommy continued, a slight sneer on his face. 'It sounds class altogether. I'd have gotten to train with Droichead's best player Billy Donovan, sure that would have been an honour. Seems like Twin Power aren't top of the pile over here anymore, is that right?'

Here we go! Aoife thought, *don't react.* The sarcasm was dripping from Tommy's words.

'Ah, Tommy, give over,' Darragh told his friend sternly.

'I'm only messing, Dar,' Tommy laughed out loud, a bit manically. 'Sure, you all knew that, didn't you? Aren't we all great buddies after we cleared up our little misunderstandings last year?'

Silence greeted him.

'I don't know about that,' Aidan muttered under his breath, kicking a stone.

Tommy had ruined the fun atmosphere in the group and Aidan was sick of his presence already. Aidan was annoyed at himself for being annoyed at Billy and Darragh's friendship and now Tommy was throwing out stupid comments. And before a final too. Would he ever just go away?

'Did you say something, Aidan?' Tommy asked.

'I said, I don't know if you really were messing,' Aidan said loudly. 'We could all do without sarcastic comments before the match. C'mon, let's go and get ready.'

The Droichead gang all started to gather their boots and water bottles and headed towards the pitch.

'Ah, that's a pity,' Tommy said as they departed, still

with the fixed grin. 'I was looking forward to chatting to you all about the Lost Cup.'

Everyone froze where they were standing.

'How do *you* know about the Lost Cup?' Aoife asked slowly.

'I didn't know it was a big secret,' Tommy said, mock innocently, hands out wide. 'Did you, Ellie?'

'Nope,' Ellie sneered. 'I reckon it's made up anyway,' she continued.

'Oh no, I'd say it's true enough all right, Ellie. The wonderful Aidan Power doesn't lie. I can't remember exactly who told me,' Tommy lied easily. 'I just heard about it yesterday. I said to myself, I can't wait to start looking for the Lost Cup with all my Droichead buddies. That might be worth money, I said to myself. Or I could get on the TV if I found it, imagine. RTÉ interviewing Tommy Doyle right here in Droichead. Can you imagine the headline? "Star Gorman player finds historic Lost Cup". I can see it now.'

Billy looked like he might get sick. Darragh shifted uncomfortably.

'Anyway, great to see you all,' Tommy winked.

'May the best team win. C'mon, Darragh.'

Darragh slunk away behind a laughing Tommy and Ellie, as Aoife and Aidan looked towards a guilty Billy, who quickly looked away.

'Droichead, let's go, time for our warm-up,' Mr Power shouted.

CHAPTER 7

'Aoife,' Sara hissed as they lined up for a quick handpassing drill. 'Who told Tommy about the Lost Cup?'

'Billy must have told Darragh, it's the only thing I can think of,' Aoife replied quickly.

'Well, it wasn't a secret!' John hissed from behind them. 'Watch out, Sara, it's your turn.'

Sara quickly grabbed the ball that was handpassed to her from Jakub, one of the forwards on the team. She ran forward, handpassing over and back at speed to Derval, who was in the line next to them.

Aoife and John were still waiting in their row. Aidan and Billy were in the row next to them, also waiting.

'The boys aren't talking,' John nudged Aoife in the back and nodded his head in the direction of Billy and Aidan.

'Oh no,' Aoife groaned. 'We can't have our two midfielders not talking to each other.'

Aoife was up next, handpassing over and back to Billy. He refused to meet her eye and uncharacteristically dropped the ball twice.

When John and Aidan had finished their turn, Mr Power called them in for the last chat before throw-in.

Billy and Aidan walked together behind the rest of the team.

'I'm sorry I told Darragh about the Lost Cup,' Billy blurted out. 'I didn't think he would tell Tommy. But I didn't know it was a secret and I didn't tell him not to tell anyone, so it's not his fault.'

'Oh, of course it's not Darragh's fault,' Aidan said bitterly.

'What's that supposed to mean?' Billy asked.

'Nothing!' Aidan snorted.

'Look, the minute Tommy started talking about it in his sneering way, I knew I shouldn't have said any-

60

thing,' Billy continued. 'I just told Darragh because it was something interesting to talk about at skills training. It wasn't a secret!'

'Well, you've ruined everything!' Aidan was shouting now and getting red in the face.

The rest of the team turned to look.

'It could have been fun!' Aidan kept shouting. 'It could have been our gang solving a mystery, but you had to get friendly with horrible *GORMAN* people.'

'Calm down, Aidan,' Billy said quietly. 'I'm only friendly with Darragh, not Tommy. We are *all* friendly with Darragh – and Maeve.'

The whole team was watching now as Aidan roared, '*GET LOST, BILLY!*'

With that he turned and walked to the team dugout.

'What in the name of goodness is going on?' Mr Power shouted, as the referee blew his whistle indicating that the match needed to start.

Donie and Kathleen motioned to Billy and Aidan to come over to them and the two boys reluctantly made their way over.

'I don't know what happened between you two,'

Donie said, 'but this stops now. We have an important match here and we need our two midfielders getting along.'

'Is that clear?' Mr Power asked sternly. 'Did you hear what Donie said, Aidan?'

'Yes,' Aidan muttered mutinously.

Billy nodded.

The referee blew her whistle and beckoned for the captains to come in for the toss.

'Aidan, off you go,' Mr Power said.

'I don't want to be captain today,' Aidan sulked.

Mr Power sighed. Time was against him. He looked around him. Billy and Aidan wouldn't look at each other, Aoife was distracted, most of the team were nudging each other and whispering. John stood silently putting on his goalie gloves.

'John, will you be our captain today?' Mr Power asked him.

'Me?' John looked up, surprised. 'Yeah, sure, I'd love to.'

'Run out there, so, like a good man for the coin toss, please,' Mr Power said. 'If we win the toss, tell the referee that we will play with the wind in the first half,' he added.

'OK, let's go, team,' Mr Power said addressing them all. 'I don't have time to say all that I was going to say. I don't know what the shouting was about and frankly I don't want to know. We have an important match here for which we are very well prepared. We need to focus.'

John rejoined the group.

'We lost the toss,' he said. 'We're playing into the wind in the first half.'

Mr Power continued his talk.

'As I was saying, we must keep focused. We're starting with the same thirteen who started in the last match. You know what's expected of you. Backs, stay tight on the player you're marking and support the midfielders. Forwards, get out in front of your markers. You've been playing very well as a team. I want that to continue,' he said, looking pointedly at Aidan and Billy. 'Darragh Cunningham in mid-field for Gorman is playing well. Billy, I want you to start off marking him, simply because you have the height advantage. We may move Aidan onto him after a while, we will see how it goes. Aidan, you start marking Ellie. I presume they will play her in midfield with Darragh.

'Aoife, centre forward as usual, moving at speed, bursting through, scoring points, that's your job. Sara, you are on fire in right corner forward. Keep it going, you can score off both legs so don't be afraid to kick with your left, OK?'

Sara nodded.

'Jennifer, David, solid in backs. Tommy Doyle will be playing corner forward for Gorman and he can kick from anywhere so mark tight. Right, let's go, folks.'

The referee blew her whistle again, impatiently this time. The Gorman team were lined up on the pitch ready to go.

'C'mon Droichead, you're late,' the referee shouted.

'Go, go,' Kathleen said urgently.

The Droichead team ran out onto the pitch and took their positions. Billy tried to make eye contact with Aidan as they ran out, but Aidan refused to meet his eye. Even lining up for the throw-in, the two of them standing side by side, they didn't say a word.

'Best of luck, lads,' Darragh grinned, standing next

to them for the throw-in for Gorman.

Aidan suddenly realised that Ellie was not the other midfielder. It was Corey Walsh. *Where's Ellie?* he wondered as the referee threw the ball in the air.

Down in her corner forward position, Sara had found Ellie. It wasn't good news. Gorman had moved Ellie into corner back, to mark Sara. This wasn't good for Droichead. Ellie was a brilliant marker, and this was a good tactical move by Gorman to try and contain Sara who had been scoring for fun in recent games.

'Oh no,' John thought to himself, from his position in goal. But he had his own problems to contend with as he saw Tommy Doyle swaggering around in the full forward position right in from of John's goal. Tina usually marked him and did an excellent job, but Tina wasn't here. That responsibility had fallen to David O'Keeffe who, while he was a good back, John wasn't sure that he fully realised how good Tommy Doyle was at popping over points.

Darragh won the throw-in for Gorman and powered up the pitch. He made a great kick pass to Tommy up front, who turned and kicked with his left leg. Point.

John kicked out the ball, aiming for Aidan on the right wing. John wasn't a fan of kicking down the middle, always to the sides. It usually worked a treat but today, Aidan uncharacteristically fumbled the ball, dropped it, and it was whipped up by Corey, the other Gorman midfielder, who passed it into Maeve, who deftly hopped, soloed, thought about kicking a point, but realising how close she was to goal, pointed her toe down and shot for goal. Boom, back of the net. John wasn't sure how it happened. Maeve had a powerful kick for sure, but he should have saved that.

'You lot are all over the place,' Tommy mocked.

'Leave it, Tommy,' Maeve cautioned. 'It's early days yet.'

John went left with the kick-out and Billy confidently caught the ball and took off. He passed to Aoife who was champing at the bit to get on the ball. She burst through the Gorman defenders with her lightning speed, and quickly popped the ball over the bar.

1-1 Gorman 0-1 Droichead

'C'mon now, Droichead,! Aoife shouted, doing her best to create some motivation in her team, as she ran back to mark the Gorman centre back, Israel, for the kick-out. Israel had no hope of winning the kick-out with Aoife stuck to him like glue. Likewise, for Darragh, with Billy hanging around him. But Aidan, who was the smallest bit off tempo today, allowed Corey an opportunity to run and win that kick-out and before Aidan knew it, Corey had passed the ball off to Maeve, who had dropped back towards the half forward line. She picked out Tommy perfectly with a brilliant kick pass. Tommy, with his uncanny knack of being in the right place at the right time, kicked the ball for a point but it went low and, as John watched in horror, it dropped down and into the top of the goal. Another goal for Gorman.

2-1 to 0-1 to Gorman now.

'Oh, man,' Tommy said, rubbing his hands in glee. 'Twin Power aren't at the races at all today. Well, one of them maybe. I don't know about the great Billy Donovan either,' he roared to make sure Billy would hear his name.

'Take no notice, Billy,' Darragh said sensibly to his

opposing player. 'It's just Tommy's way to play mind games.'

'Oh, I know that by now,' Billy said. 'I don't care, water off a duck's back to me.'

'Yeah, but it does work on some people,' Darragh replied.

Don't I know it! Billy thought, looking at Aidan's thunderous face, and at John, very flustered in goals.

'John!' Aoife shouted, 'Over here!'

She had made a run down the field to win the kick-out. Aoife's speed got her to places that she had no right to be.

Israel was still trying to follow her when she won the kick-out and worked it up the field. Sara had finally broken free of Ellie; she received the pass from Aoife, turned to her left side, as Ellie reached her on the right, and kicked over the bar with her left leg.

'That's more like it!' Aoife roared.

'Yeah, c'mon, Droichead,' Billy echoed, trying to rally the troops.

Surprised, Aoife looked at Billy. It was usually Aidan who was organising, cajoling, talking to his teammates in the middle of the field. But not today.

It struck Aoife that her superstar brother had been largely anonymous on the pitch, which was so unlike him.

By half time, Droichead had kicked two more points, one each for Aoife and Billy. Sara was really struggling to get free of Ellie, and Aidan was moving slower than anyone had ever seen him.

The half time score was 2-02 to Gorman 0-04 Droichead. Gorman were winning by four points.

CHAPTER 8

'OK, team,' Mr Power started. 'We are doing OK. Gorman are strong, as we knew they would be. But we're only four points down and while they have scored two goals, they aren't scoring that many points. We have four scores each. We are very much still in this match and we have the wind in the second half.'

'We're making some small changes in the second half,' Donie continued. 'Aoife, we are swapping you into midfield and Aidan into centre-forward.'

Aidan's head dropped.

'Aidan, this isn't a bad reflection on you,' Kathleen said. 'Aoife is dropping back there anyway and winning kick-outs so we'll leave her at it, and we want you to kick some scores, as we know you can.'

'Use your speed, Aidan, OK?' Donie said pointedly.

'OK,' Aidan muttered.

'Billy, you are doing well on Darragh,' Mr Power said. 'Don't get overly confident, he will have his purple patch, mark my words.'

'Sara, I know it's hard with Ellie marking you. It's a compliment to you and your skill that they put her marking you. It's literally her only job on the pitch. But keep making runs, tire her out, OK? You never know what might happen,' Kathleen said.

'OK,' Sara said confidently.

'Finally,' Mr Power said, 'Tommy and Maeve up front for Gorman are very dangerous. David and Jennifer, you have to be so tight on them. My mission for you both, and the rest of the backs, plus John in goals, is no more goals, that's your challenge, OK?'

'OK, Mr Power,' John smacked his gloves together determinedly. 'You can count on us.'

'Right, let's go win this final,' Mr Power said. 'Let's get back out there, give it everything!'

Aidan tried to give himself a talking to as he jogged

out to the centre forward position.

Cop on now, Aidan, forget about Billy, forget about Darragh. So what if they are friends? They're not going to forget about me, of course not. But what if they do? What if they team up and find the Lost Cup without me? That was my idea. What if Tommy helps them? What if Billy becomes friendly with Tommy as well. Then who will I have? Aoife, but she will be off with Sara and Tina. John, he is so busy with the farming. I will be all alone. Oh my God, Aidan, do you hear yourself? This is ridiculous. And he shook his head at his own silliness. *They are my friends, my sister, my team, this is so silly. I need to stop worrying and play football.*

'Aidan!'

He was woken from his reverie by Aoife's voice. She had the ball and was looking to pass to him. Usually, she wouldn't need to call him, he would just seem to know where she was and where she needed him to be. He felt Israel, the Gorman centre back's, shoulder next to his, his breath so close. Aidan needed to move. He made a run, but Israel was still with him. He saw Aoife, unsure of what to do, she had hopped and soloed, she was stuck, she needed to pass. She was about to handpass to him; he could see it in her movements. He tried to run again to get free, but Israel was still there next to him. Quick as a flash, Aoife looked up, saw Billy free further up the pitch and delivered him a perfect kick pass. Billy turned and popped the ball over the bar for a point.

Aidan felt bereft. He just couldn't get into the game. It was great that Billy had scored but he, Aidan, needed to do more.

Sara followed up with another score and now there was only a two-point gap.

But then as Mr Power had predicted, Darragh found a way to get around Billy and showed how dangerous he could be, by scoring twice in three minutes. Back to a four-point difference.

Ten minutes left on the clock and Aidan felt something shift inside him. He really needed to start playing here, he was letting his team down. He ran at speed, surprising Israel. John looked up just in time to see Aidan free, one of the first times all day he had been. John quickly kicked the ball out, a perfect pass to Aidan. Aidan took off up the pitch, sensing for the first time all day that Aoife was with him. Without so much as a glance, he knew she was running on, he felt her presence, handpassed to her. They expertly worked the ball up the field together. As they neared the goal, Aoife grabbed the ball, dropped it from her right hand, pointed her toe low down and put the ball into the back of the net. *GOAL!*

Now Droichead were only one point behind and suddenly it was anyone's game.

A few cagey minutes followed with bad wides from each side. Then Darragh, in a moment of footballing genius, leapt higher off the ground than anyone had ever seen and caught the ball firmly with both hands. As he dropped back down, Billy tried to tackle him, but Darragh was too quick. He was gone and before Droichead knew what was happening, Tommy had the ball in his hands, and he was going for goal.

Remembering what Mr Power had said about no goals, Jennifer and David, the full backs, both tried to tackle him, but Tommy was so nimble that he got around both of them. It was up to John in goals to stop him. John looked firmly at Tommy and saw that he was about to shoot. He slid his body along the ground towards the ball as it left Tommy's foot, but was just a fraction too late and he watched in dismay as the ball sailed over his feet and into the back of the net. As he watched the ball fly past him, he was suddenly aware of a cracking sound and a pain ripping through his ankle. Tommy, having kicked the ball, had slipped and followed through with his boots making contact with John's ankle.

John roared in pain as Tommy scrambled to stand up and protest his innocence. 'I slipped, ref,' were the first words to leave his mouth.

The referee had just blown the final whistle. Tommy's goal kick was the final kick of the game and the Gorman team started jumping around in delight, celebrating at winning the league. Droichead were distraught.

All celebrations came to an abrupt halt as the players realised the seriousness of John's injury. The Gorman coaches quickly ushered their players away, Tommy still loudly claiming it was an accident.

The Droichead gang rushed to their friend's aid. John was crying on the ground as Mr Power and Kathleen knelt next to him trying to assess his injury. Mr Power turned to Aidan and Aoife.

'Aoife, run over to the stand, please and ask Tina's mam to come over,' he asked his daughter calmly.

Tina's mam was a GP in Carrick and would surely know what to do.

'Aidan, will you bring the team back to the dugout to give us a bit of space, please. Billy you too, keep them all together and we'll be over in a minute.'

Donie started ushering the players away and they reluctantly moved toward the side of the pitch.

Tina and her mam were walking rapidly towards the pitch as Aoife ran towards them.

Do they need my help, Aoife?' Tina's mam asked.

'Yes, please, Dr O'Shea. John is really hurt.'

Half an hour later, John was lifted off the pitch by several parents under the watchful instruction of Dr O'Shea. She thought that he had broken his ankle. He was to be brought to the hospital in Carrick for an X-ray.

Aoife, Aidan, Billy, Sara and Tina patted him on the arm as he went past.

'We'll call to see you tomorrow, John,' they promised.

John tried and failed to raise a grin, pain etched all

over his face.

The cup presentation had been delayed until John was tended to, but now Droichead had to face the Gorman celebrations. They clapped for their rivals even though their hearts weren't in it. But they knew it was the right thing to do. They had been on the other side of this in the Star Schools final last year.

Slowly, they all walked over and shook hands with the Gorman players and admired their county medals.

'Great game,' Aoife said as she shook hands with Maeve. 'You were amazing.'

'Right back at you,' Maeve said. 'Was Aidan OK?' she whispered. 'He usually plays better than that.'

'Erm, I think he felt a bit sick,' Aoife replied, loyal as always to her twin.

'Tommy is mouthing about how Billy and Aidan are not talking,' Maeve whispered back.

'I wouldn't take any notice of Tommy Doyle,' Aoife smiled.

Don't worry, I don't!' Maeve smiled back.

Sara and Tina came over and joined Maeve and Aoife.

'I should have played,' Tina hissed at Aoife, out of earshot of the others. 'I might have been able to mark Tommy and have stopped him from taking that awful shot on John.'

'Oh, Tina don't think like that,' Aoife said hugging her friend. 'I *do* wish you would come back and play though. We'll chat about this later, OK?'

They quickly changed the subject as Billy, Aidan and Darragh joined the group.

'Well done, Darragh,' the Droichead gang chorused again.

'Ah thanks, lads,' Darragh replied. 'I just feel like we shouldn't be celebrating when poor John is in hospital.'

'Ah look, you deserve the celebration,' Aidan said, sensible Aidan returning.

'Aidan's right,' Billy agreed, and they exchanged a friendly look.

Phew! Aoife thought. *Maybe this will all blow over.*

Right then, who walked past, only Tommy and Ellie with trouble written all over their faces.

'Hard luck, Droichead,' Tommy shouted, a big smile on his face. 'It's only fair, I suppose, when you lot robbed us of the Star Schools final. What goes around, comes around and all that.'

'Leave it, Tommy,' Darragh groaned. 'Let's just go. Sorry, lads,' he said to his Droichead friends.

Tommy wasn't done.

'Bad day at the office for you, Aidan,' he smirked. 'I mean, I get it. It must have been hard to play a decent game of football, knowing that your best buddy, the great Billy Donovan, fancies your sister.'

'What!' Billy roared, face bright red, 'I never said that.'

'He's only rising you,' Darragh cautioned. 'Take no notice, it's rubbish.'

'What are you talking about, Tommy,' Tina said sternly. 'We're all friends here in Droichead, boys and girls, there's no need to be going around embarrassing and upsetting people.'

'Exactly, Tina,' Darragh continued. 'Stop being weird, Tommy. I've had enough of this. Talk about ruining a good day for Gorman.'

But Aoife had burst into tears and run off. Aidan, face like thunder, snarled at Tommy.

'Don't you come near Droichead, Tommy Doyle,

we've all had enough of your poison.'

'Ah, I'll have to call over,' Tommy laughed. 'Aren't we all going to find the Lost Cup together? Or maybe I'll just find it myself first.'

With that, leaving carnage behind him, he turned and left, Ellie cackling as they went.

'You've single-handedly dismantled their little gang, Tommy,' she laughed as they high-fived each other. 'They're nearly all fighting now.'

'Which means I've taken down Droichead football team too,' Tommy grinned. 'All in a day's work.'

CHAPTER 9

Two weeks passed in Droichead Beag. April turned into May, spring into summer. The weather seemed to be going in reverse. The unseasonably warm weather, which had lasted for the first two weeks of April, ended the morning after the Droichead under 12s lost their final against Gorman. Two weeks of miserable, cold, wet weather followed.

Things were not good in the Amber Fields gang. The bad weather meant few matches after school on the green in Amber Fields. Football training in Droichead GAA was cancelled the week after the final, and then cancelled again the following week due to harsh weather.

Preparations were well under way in school for the

sixth-class graduation. Most of the Amber Fields gang were looking forward to moving on to secondary school in September. However, the recent increase in tension with the Gorman gang was making some of them nervous about going to secondary school in Carrick together. Aidan, in particular, kept thinking about how horrible it was going to be having to look at Tommy Doyle every day in school.

Things weren't great in school in Droichead as it was. Aidan and Billy weren't talking, despite sitting next to each other in class. Aoife and Billy were talking, when they had to, but it was awkward like it never had been before. John had indeed broken his ankle. He was back in school, but on crutches for the next few weeks and unable to play any sport.

Sara, however, was happy. She was delighted to have her grandfather staying on his holidays from Poland and he was very interested in learning all about Gaelic games. Tina was also starting to talk about football again, which was positive.

Finally on Sunday 2 May, the rain stopped, and the sun shone.

Tina knocked on the door of the Powers' house,

bright and early, her dog Max straining on his lead next to her. Aoife looked out the window and hurriedly ran down the stairs, shouting to her mam that she was going for a walk with Tina and Max.

'Is Aidan going with you?' Mrs Power shouted back from where she was kicking a ball around with Clare in the back garden.

'Aidan, are you coming for a walk with me and Tina?' Aoife roared up the stairs.

'Can we all stop shouting?' Mr Power walked out onto the landing at the top of the stairs.

'Oh, hi, Tina, hi, Max,' he said smiling at the visitors in the doorway.

Aidan stuck his head out of his bedroom. 'No, you two head off. I'm going over to Nana and Grandad's in a minute,' he said.

'Fine, suit yourself, we're heading to the new walk, down by the river,' Aoife said. 'See you all later.'

The girls called on Sara in number 4 Amber Fields and she joined them for the walk, after introducing them to her grandfather, Stanisław Novak. He was delighted to meet the girls and told them that he was looking forward to seeing them play ladies' Gaelic football very soon.

'I told him that we are playing Carrick at the end of the month, he can't wait,' Sara said as the trio left Amber Fields and headed through the village towards the bridge and the river walk.

'Oh, that's going to be a hard match,' Aoife groaned, 'I hope he won't be disappointed. Carrick are really good.'

'They are, but we are doing really well too, Aoife,' Tina said. 'We're only a new club and we've won loads of matches!'

'I love that you are saying "we" Tina,' Sara said, smiling. 'Does this mean you might come back playing?'

'I think I will,' Tina said. 'Definitely with the girls' team. I'm still not sure about playing with the boys with Droichead GAA.'

'Why don't you want to, do you know?' Aoife asked gently.

'I'm not really sure,' Tina replied honestly, tightening Max's lead as a car went past. 'It's hard to explain. I just feel a bit embarrassed. I feel that maybe people are thinking I look funny in my shorts because I'm tall and that they are thinking I'm not a good footballer.' She shrugged.

'Well, can I just say that you are an excellent footballer and that's plain to see,' Aoife replied.

'Uh, obviously!' Sara nodded. 'That was never in doubt. We are much weaker in the backs without you.'

'Also,' Aoife continued, 'my mam said to me recently that everyone is more worried about themselves and what they look like than worrying about what other people look like in shorts or jerseys.'

'I wish I was as tall as you, Tina,' Sara added. 'You can catch the ball so high up!'

'But I do understand how things can be embarrassing,' Aoife said sadly.

'Do you mean what Tommy said at the end of the final?' Sara asked her friend. 'About Billy fancying you?'

'Yeah,' Aoife grimaced, 'Billy was so embarrassed. It was cringe.'

'What if it is true, what if he does fancy you?' Tina asked slowly.

'Ah no, he doesn't. I don't like that kind of talk.

It felt so weird. I just want us all to be friends. It makes me feel so self-conscious when Tommy talks like that. I start wondering was I acting like I fancied Billy. But I know I wasn't, we're the same as always, just friends! Anyway, *that's* embarrassing, playing football with boys Tina, that's not embarrassing.'

'I suppose when you put it like that,' Tina laughed, 'maybe it's not!'

'So, we're agreed?' Aoife asked. 'We'll support each other and get back to playing football and having fun. Girl Power!'

'If we have Girl Power and Twin Power, we will be flying!' Sara laughed.

'Agreed,' Tina said firmly. 'I promise not to make any embarrassing comments to you about Billy and will shut it down fast if anyone else so much as dares to whisper it!'

'Same here,' Sara nodded quickly 'and I promise to tell you if your football shorts are too short, Tina!'

The girls descended into a fit of laughter as they walked under the bridge and started along the river walk.

'Seriously though,' Sara said. 'I do feel a bit like our

Amber Fields gang is breaking up and that makes me sad.'

'Ah it's not, Sara,' Tina reassured her friend.

'Billy and Aidan aren't talking,' Sara protested. 'Billy and Aoife are being weird to each other. We hardly see John because of his broken ankle. We don't see you at training or playing in the green, Tina. I just want things to go back to the way they were!' Sara finished.

'Sara has a point,' Aoife admitted. 'Maybe we do need to work at fixing this before things get any worse. I need to be the Aidan in this situation and be practical and try and sort things.'

'I have fixed one problem' Tina said. 'I'll come back playing football in the green. If I feel like I'm enjoying that, then maybe I'll go back playing with Droichead. I will *definitely* go back playing on the Droichead/Gorman girls' team. I really miss that.'

'OK, that's one problem solved,' Aoife said. 'If Tina can be brave, then so can I. I'll just start talking to Billy like normal again, forget Tommy ever said anything.'

'Em, maybe you should talk to Billy about what

was said,' Sara asked.

'Are you out of your mind, Sara? No way. You said yourself, you want things back to the way they were, so that's what I'll do: pretend like nothing ever happened.'

'OK, have it your way,' Sara sighed. 'The biggest problem,' she continued 'is Aidan and Billy.'

'Yeah, that will take a bit of fixing,' Tina said.

'Yup,' Aoife groaned. 'Oh, look,' she said suddenly, 'there's my nana and grandad's farm, we were talking so much, I didn't realise how far we had walked. Let's call in. They always have yummy cake. Aidan might be there too.'

The trio of girls and Max arrived to a warm welcome in Joe and Mary Power's farm.

'Ah, my favourite girls,' Mary hugged them all when they came in. 'Look, the lovely Max, isn't he a dote? Come here until I give you a bit of ham, Max.'

Max was thrilled with the attention from Mary and licked her hand repeatedly.

Will ye have a bit of cake?' Mary asked the girls

'Yes, please,' they chorused.

'Where are Aidan and Grandad?' Aoife asked.

'They are out fixing a fence I think,' Mary said. 'That twin of yours is in bad form, Aoife, we need to sort him out. He's like a lost soul without Billy Donovan next to him.'

'We were just saying the same thing, Nana,' Aoife replied. 'Nana, did Aidan ask you about the Lost Cup?' she continued.

Mary turned away from the table suddenly and busied herself with wiping down a sideboard.

'He did, love, but I told him I don't know anything about that.'

'Are you sure?' Aoife asked.

'Ah yeah, sure aren't I a townie from Carrick,' Mary laughed.

'But Carrick were part of Coyle Gaels too, Nana,' Aoife persisted. 'Wasn't it Coyle Gaels that won the cup, the cup that was lost? Didn't anyone in Carrick ever talk about it when you were younger?'

'Not that I remember,' Mary said quickly. 'Girls, I really should help Grandad with the fence. Will ye sort yourselves out with some cake? Here it is.' With that, Mary was gone.

'Your Nana really doesn't want to talk about the

Lost Cup,' Sara said after Mary had moved quickly out the door.

'Uh huh,' Aoife said. 'I'm getting interested now. She knows more than she's letting on.'

Later that evening at home, Aoife told Aidan about their Nana's reluctance to talk about the Lost Cup.

'Grandad was exactly the same,' Aidan exclaimed. 'He buttoned up straight away. Usually you can't stop Grandad talking, he'd talk for Ireland.'

'Aidan, I think there really might be a mystery here.'

'Me too,' Aidan grinned.

'I think the Amber Fields gang might be the ones to solve it,' Aoife said, sounding Aidan out.

'Hmm, well the two of us maybe.'

'OK, we'll see,' Aoife nodded.

CHAPTER 10

Coincidentally, the twins weren't the only ones thinking about the Lost Cup.

'Aidan, did you find out any more about the mystery of the Lost Cup?' Ms Casey asked the following morning in school.

'No, *a mhúinteoir*,' Aidan replied. 'I asked my nana and grandad, but they couldn't remember anything about it. I asked my mam and dad also. They thought we had a book about the War of Independence and then the Civil War in Carrick and the surrounding areas like Droichead, but they couldn't find it.'

'Which is weird,' Aoife chimed in, 'because our dad is very organised, and he couldn't understand where the book had gone.'

'Hmm,' Ms Casey was thoughtful. 'I think I know the book that you mean. It's an old book, it was written by a local historian from Droichead. There is surely a copy in the school somewhere. Leave it with me, I will have a look.

'Now, class, our trip to Croke Park is just three weeks away, at the end of May. I gave you some history homework last night about the GAA during the War of Independence because I want you to have some knowledge before you go into the GAA Museum. Firstly, can anyone tell me when the War of Independence took place in Ireland?'

Tina's hand shot up.

'It was from January 1919 to July 1921, *a mhúinteoir*.'

'Very good, Tina. Now, John, you have been quiet today. I know you are interested in modern history. Tell me, why did the War of Independence happen in Ireland?'

'Erm,' John looked up blankly. 'Because we wanted to be free of the British?'

'Well, yes, John, that's the crux of the matter, I suppose,' Ms Casey agreed.

'We wanted to rule our own country,' Aidan added, 'to be a republic.'

'Yes, that's right, Aidan,' Ms Casey confirmed.

'Was it because of Bloody Sunday, miss?' Billy asked.

'Bloody Sunday happened during the War of Independence, Billy,' Ms Casey replied. 'It happened in November 1920. You will see an exhibition about it when we go on our school tour to Croke Park and the GAA Museum.

'In general, boys and girls, the GAA tried to stay neutral during the Easter Rising and the War of Independence. But many of its members participated in the struggle for freedom. In fact, in 1918, the GAA was declared a dangerous organisation by the British and Gaelic games were banned. But on 4 August, over 54,000 GAA members defied the ban and played games at a designated time of 3pm throughout the country. This day was known as Gaelic Sunday.'

'Look, Aidan!' Ms Casey announced triumphantly,

later that day, as the bell rang, and the class filed out. 'I found that book in the school library at lunchtime. You can take it home tonight and have a read of it. Let me know what you find out. There are two chapters all about the GAA at the time of the Civil War as well.'

'Thanks so much, Ms Casey.'

Aidan's face lit up with delight.

After school, the six of the Amber Fields gang made their way slowly along the short walk home from school. They were walking slowly as John was with them, for the first time since he had broken his ankle. He was still on crutches, but he was used to them now and able for short walks.

'I have to say, credit where it is due, Ms Casey isn't so bad after all. That history class was very interesting,' Tina started.

'You're right, Tina,' Aidan agreed. 'She seems extremely interested in the Lost Cup, which is great. She gave me this book that might help solve the mystery,' he continued holding up the history book that Ms Casey had given to him,

'Well, I'm just so glad I can stay in the village with

you all this evening,' John smiled. 'It was getting boring going home every day. I was even starting to miss calving season.'

'That *is* bad!' Sara laughed.

'At least it has been raining for the past two weeks,' John continued, 'so I didn't miss much here, or did I?'

'No, nothing much,' Tina replied. 'I'm back playing football with the girls' team. We have a big match tomorrow night against Carrick.'

'That's great, Tina,' John grinned. 'We can make our big comebacks together for Droichead GAA in time for the championship!'

'I'm thinking about it, 'Tina said, but she smiled, and Aoife had a good feeling.

'That would be fab, Tina,' Sara smiled.

Aoife nodded in agreement. 'We can warm up together, the three of us,' she grinned at her friend.

'Aidan, Billy, how are we fixed for the championship?' John asked.

'I don't know, John,' Aidan shrugged. 'It's not starting till July or August. We haven't had training in two weeks because the weather has been so bad. I haven't thought much about it, to be honest.'

'What?' John half-shouted. 'Have I entered an alternate universe? In what world is Aidan Power not thinking about the under–12 county championship? It's the biggest competition of the year.'

'It might be our chance to get revenge on Gorman,' Aoife added.

'Yeah, that too,' John added, 'that's the spirit, Aoife. What's wrong with the rest of you?'

'*I'm* excited about it,' Sara said defensively. 'I'm just busy at the moment, playing with the girls' team and explaining Gaelic games to Dziadek Staś every day!'

'Fair enough, Sara,' John replied. 'What about you, Billy? How's the skills practice going?'

'Yeah, its grand,' Billy said quietly. 'The competition is in a few weeks, just after the school tour actually.'

'And what about the championship? John asked accusingly.

'I suppose we'll give it a lash,' Billy responded.

'Ah, come on, lads,' John said, exasperated. 'Aoife, will you talk sense into these lads? This is the biggest competition of the year. OK, Gorman beat us in the league and Tommy broke my ankle, but forget that, the championship is a bigger competition and it's totally up for grabs. Ourselves and Gorman should be the best teams in it, there's every chance we'll meet them in a final again. We need to get ourselves right and get our heads in the game for this.'

'All right, John, point taken,' Billy grinned, realising now how passionately his friend felt about this.

'Let's meet here for a match on the green in half an hour,' Aoife said. 'Training starts now. John, you can be the referee.'

'Now you're talking,' John said, rubbed his hands together.

'Count me in,' Tina nodded.

'And me,' Sara smiled.

'Billy, what about you?' Aoife asked, thinking back to her chat with Tina and Sara and getting a good feeling that she could talk normally to Billy again.

Billy looked up, shocked but happy to see Aoife talk directly to him. After all the weirdness of the past two weeks, things felt almost normal again.

'Sure, I'll be out,' he smiled

'Aidan?' Aoife asked.

'I have to read this book, but I can spare half an hour,' he smiled.

'Right, see you all shortly,' Aoife said. 'C'mon John, let's go into our house and let's have a nice, toasted sandwich first.'

She hadn't failed to notice that Aidan and Billy still were not talking directly to each other. Come to think of it, she hadn't even seen Aidan playing FIFA online the past few nights. He usually could be heard shouting excitedly during matches with Billy, John and Darragh.

'John,' she whispered when Aidan was out of ear-shot. 'Were you and the lads playing FIFA online last night?'

'Erm, let me think. Oh yeah, we were, I was Man Utd and I beat Billy, we definitely were.'

'Was Aidan playing?' Aoife asked.

'No, now that you mention it, he wasn't,' John said. 'Darragh was on alright, and we sent Aidan a few messages to come online, but he never did.'

Aoife frowned as John sat down at the kitchen table with Aidan.

CHAPTER 11

The following evening, Aoife excitedly pulled her Droichead/Gorman gear out of her wardrobe and busied herself with getting ready for their big match against Carrick. Aoife absolutely loved playing football with the newly formed girls' team She had often worried about where she would she play football after under 12s.

GAA rules state that girls can play Gaelic football with boys only up to under 12s. They can of course play ladies' football at any age group. But there had been no ladies' football club in Droichead until a few months ago. Aoife always thought she would have to go to Carrick ladies' football club and while that would have been fine, it wouldn't have been the same as putting on her own parish jersey, the place where she was from, where she had grown up.

Thankfully, last year, due to the large number of girls playing football in the area, a group of people, including her mam, her fifth-class teacher Ms Kelly, Annie Doyle from Gorman and of course, local legend Jenny McCarthy, who was a county player, had set up a brand-new ladies' football club, called Droichead Beag/Gorman Ladies' Football Club.

Aoife had thought that combining with Gorman players would cause problems because of the intense rivalry, but in fact, it was working out very well.

Aoife loved playing on a team with Maeve from Gorman, who had become a good friend. And while she didn't get on with Ellie Ryan at all, Aoife had a good football brain and knew how a strong and ferocious player like Ellie was a huge asset to their team. In fairness to Ellie, she didn't mess around on the pitch and had no problem passing to Droichead players at all. She wanted to win.

This match tonight against Carrick was the first time they had played them. Carrick were county champions and formidable opponents.

The girls were playing them in the ladies' under-12 county league. Winning the league was probably out of Droichead/Gorman's reach in this, their first year playing, but a good result against Carrick would really show that they meant business.

Aoife threw on her blue and red shorts. The club had taken the red from the black and red of Droichead and the blue from the blue and white of Gorman and combined them to make a lovely red and blue club kit.

'Aoife, are you ready?' her mam called up the stairs.

'Yup,' Aoife said, running down the stairs, 'let's do this!'

They walked quickly over to the Droichead pitch where today's match was taking place. Sometimes they played on the Gorman pitch but joint club or not, Aoife was always secretly happier playing in Droichead. It was where she belonged.

Aoife's mam, Annie Doyle and Ms Kelly were the selectors and coaches for the team, and they quickly called out the positions, handed out the jerseys and got a quick and efficient warm-up going.

'I'm so glad I'm back,' Tina grinned as they practised their kicking.

'So are we!' Sara and Aoife said in unison.

'Me too,' Maeve chimed in.

'We could do with your help in the backs all right,' Ellie said grudgingly. 'Especially against Carrick.'

'Look at our fan club,' Sara laughed.

Aidan, Billy and John were sitting in the stand. Darragh and Tommy sat a few rows back with a few of the other Gorman lads on their team.

Sitting in the front row were Sara's parents, the Novaks, and her grandfather, Stanisław Novak.

'C'mon, Droichead/Gorman,' John roared, waving down at them.

The girls laughed. Aoife caught Billy's eye and blushed. *What was that about?* she thought mortified. *C'mon, Aoife, focus*, she said to herself as she headed towards the middle of the pitch for the throw-in. Aoife was always midfield for the ladies' club and today was no exception.

The hour that followed was a magnificent game of football. Both sides gave it everything and the brand-new club came so close to snatching a victory from Carrick. In the end, it finished a draw, and everyone agreed that it was a fair result. Droichead/Gorman were really impressing everyone in their very first year of existence.

The Droichead/Gorman girls shook hands with their Carrick opponents and then collapsed in a heap on the grass near the dugout. It was hot and they gulped water and lay back, bodies spent; they had given it their all.

Their supporters wandered over after a while, Billy and Aidan walking slowly to stay in time with John on his crutches.

'How's the leg, John?' Darragh asked, as he and Tommy and the Gorman lads passed the Droichead boys.

'Getting there, Darragh, thanks. I'll be back in time for the championship.'

'That's great news,' Tommy smirked.

Aidan eyed him suspiciously. Could he never stop being sarcastic?

'How's the skills training going?' Tommy kept talking, directing his question to Billy. 'Not a hope you'll beat my man Darragh here, he can kick a point from anywhere on the pitch.'

'Ah, stop, Tommy,' Darragh nudged his friend, 'give it a rest.'

'Those girls are good though,' Tommy kept going. 'Especially Ellie. She brings another level to the team. I suppose your lot aren't bad either. Twin Power 1 can run anyway.'

'She can do more than run,' Aidan snarled.

'And her name is Aoife,' Billy added.

'Sticking up for his girlfriend,' Tommy laughed.

'Leave it,' John cautioned as he saw the cross faces on Billy and Aidan, as they arrived close to where the girls were still sitting on the grass.

'Girls and boys,' Aoife's mam said suddenly, addressing the gathered crowd. 'We are honoured to have a famous sportsperson in our midst today. Sara's grandfather, Stanisław Novak would like to have a few words with you all.'

Sara looked on in surprise as her grandad stepped out from behind Mrs Power.

'Hello, girls,' he said slowly. 'My English is not too good, but I'll try my best. I wanted to come over here and tell you how brilliant you were today. I was so impressed watching you play.'

'Mr Novak is a former professional soccer player for Poland,' Annie Doyle said. 'He has also coached lots of soccer teams in Poland since he retired, both club teams and with the national squad.'

'I have wanted to come to Ireland for a long time,' Mr Novak continued. 'Sara is the first woman in our family to play sport. When her father told me how much she loved Gaelic football, I started to read about it and learn about your national sports. I also watched videos of you playing that my son sent to me.

'Poland is a little behind Ireland in terms of women's participation in team sports like soccer. I have been so inspired by Sara and all of you, that I am coming out of retirement and taking up a new challenge in the autumn, as coach of the women's soccer team in our local town in Poland.'

'Wow, Dziadek Staś that's amazing.' Sara hugged him. 'So that's your new challenge?'

'Yes, that is it, Sara,' Stanisław beamed. 'But first, I am here for another few weeks and I would love to take you girls for a training session. I do not know all the skills of Gaelic football, but I could do some fitness work with you, and you could teach me the skills. Would you like that?'

'Yes, please,' the girls all chorused.

'Would you take us for a session as well?' Aidan asked softly. 'There are boys and girls on the Droichead GAA team?'

'I would like this very much,' Mr Novak said. 'If that is OK with your coaches?

Mr Power nodded. 'We would be honoured,' he said.

'I was a bit confused about mixed teams in Gaelic games,' Mr Novak continued. 'But I am starting to see the benefits of it. I have read lots of research and in the UK for example, boys and girls can play soccer together up to under 17. You boys and girls of Ireland are teaching this old coach lots of new tricks!'

CHAPTER 12

May continued with no dramatics. Aoife and Aidan spent a lot of time down on the new greenway. They often brought a ball with them and kicked around in the clearing that wasn't too far from Nana and Grandad's farm. There were picnic tables there now, and Aoife sometimes brought her sketchpad and sat down to draw some pictures. Sometimes Billy came with them, but things still weren't right between himself and Aidan. Aidan knew he was being stubborn, but he couldn't help but feel betrayed by Billy telling Darragh about the Lost Cup. Then there was the matter of those comments about Aoife. Aidan knew that he should talk to Billy. It was just so weird hearing Tommy make comments like that when he was talking about his best friend and twin sister. Aidan wanted everything to go back to the way it was with everyone hanging around together and having a laugh.

The most annoying thing was that Billy seemed to be perfectly fine. Back in the spring, Billy had been anxious and nervous when he told the twins that he had won the skills competition ahead of them. Now, he seemed on top of the world, laughing and joking with Darragh, while Aidan felt miserable. That loss to Gorman in the league final really stung and without having Billy to chat to, Aidan felt miserable. Aidan couldn't help feeling hurt that Billy was doing fine. Aidan had always thought that he was as friendly with Darragh as Billy was. He liked having Darragh as a friend, he was sound. But now it seemed like Darragh was friendlier with Billy than he was with Aidan, and Aidan wasn't sure that he liked that idea at all.

Today, the twins watched intently as the people working on the greenway began uncovering an old stone structure near the picnic-table area.

'What's that?' Aidan asked Matt, a local man who

he knew had a big interest in history and who was directing some of the workers.

'That, young Mr Power, is a lime kiln,' Matt said smiling.

'What's a lime kiln?' Aoife asked. 'I've heard of them but I'm not sure what they are?'

'Well, Aoife, as you know, the land around here is very boggy,' Matt started to explain. 'Which means that it is not good soil for growing crops. It's because it's too acidic you see. But if you put lime on acidic soil, it makes it more alkaline and makes it three or four times better for growing crops.

'Over a hundred years ago, the only way to get lime was to bring it up from the lower parish area, which has alkaline soil and has lots of limestone. It would be in rocks. Then the farmers would use the kiln to heat these limestone rocks to extremely high temperatures, which would turn them into dust. This dust could then be spread on the soil to improve it. Lots of farmers had lime kilns. I knew that there was one here near your grandparents' farm, this one here, but that it had fallen into disrepair.'

'So did this kiln belong to the Power family?'

Aidan asked, curious.

'I'm not sure about that, Aidan, I'm still trying to figure it out. We are going to restore it so that people can admire it when they are on the greenway walk. We will put up a sign about the history of it, when I fully figure it out, that is!'

'That's cool,' Aoife said.

'Will you paint a picture of it for us, Aoife?' Matt continued. 'I have heard that you're a very talented painter.'

'Maybe,' Aoife smiled. 'C'mon, Aidan, we need to go home and get ready for our school tour.'

CHAPTER 13

Excitement was high as sixth class poured into the bus the next morning for their school tour to Croke Park and the GAA museum the following morning.

There were five seats across the back of the bus and the Amber Fields gang quickly commandeered them as well as the row of two in front of them so that John could stretch out his leg. His cast had been taken off two days previously, but he still needed to rest and do lots of physio and exercise to get right for the championship.

But John was determined to be back at football by the end of the summer. He was adhering exactly to the exercise plan that the physio had given him.

As the bus rolled out of the school carpark, Aidan pulled out the book about the War of Independence in Carrick and the surrounding area that Ms Casey had given him.

'Ah, look at the teacher's pet,' John joked.

'Leave it off, John,' Aidan retorted. 'I haven't had much time to read this, and I want to have a look at it before we get to the museum in Croke Park, so that I know what I'm looking for.'

'What *are* you looking for?' Tina asked.

'Information about the Lost Cup,' Aidan replied.

'He is a man on a mission,' Aoife laughed.

'I like this,' Sara smiled. 'We must all help Aidan to find out anything we can in the museum about the Lost Cup.'

'Yeah, imagine if it's real and we find out where its hidden,' Billy grinned.

'That would be so cool,' Aidan agreed.

Aoife felt a thaw starting between the two friends and began to hope.

Three hours later, with 'Olé Olé' ringing in their ears from the constant singing, the fifth and sixth classes of Droichead Beag hopped out of the bus and started walking in the direction of Croke Park, carefully guided by Ms Casey, Ms Kelly and several other teachers who had come along to help out.

'Did you know,' Billy started, 'that Croke Park is the third biggest stadium in Europe in terms of capacity?'

'Really?' Aoife was woken from her reverie.

'Yup, only Barcelona's Nou Camp and Wembley can fit more people.'

'That's really cool,' Sara exclaimed.

'How do you know that, Billy?' Ms Casey, who was in earshot, asked.

'I was reading up a bit about Croke Park last night,' Billy blushed.

'Good man,' Ms Casey smiled. 'What else did you learn?'

'I learned that Croke Park can fit 83,200 people, *a mhúinteor*,' Billy continued. 'It has been used since 1891 for Gaelic games.'

'I am impressed,' Ms Casey replied.

'You'll be getting a job as a tour guide here next, Billy,' Tina laughed.

'Boys and girls, here we are.'

'Wow!!!'

The children looked up in awe at the sheer size of the magnificent stadium. They quickly moved towards the museum entrance, which was in the Cusack Stand. Noticing the club wall outside the museum, they scrambled to find Droichead Beag GAA. The club wall had the crest of every GAA club in the country on it, as well as the clubs in England, USA, Europe, Australia, Asia and more besides.

'Look, Polish GAA clubs!' Sara exclaimed.

'Show me,' Aoife ran and looked at where her friend was pointing.

'That's amazing!' Aoife said. 'Look, there are even GAA clubs in Japan!'

'I found Droichead Beag GAA,' John shouted. 'Woohoo, first person to find it!'

'Who can find Gorman?' Ms Kelly grinned.

'What do we want to find that for, miss?' Aidan laughed.

'Look, I found Carrick!'

This continued for a while until a tour guide greeted them warmly and brought them inside.

The children were very distracted by all the books

and gifts in the shop.

'Look, Croke Park fridge magnets!' Tina squealed.

They were swiftly moved along to the tour starting point by the teachers.

'Right, tour of the stadium first,' Ms Casey announced, 'then we are going to the museum. Listen to the tour guide; off we go.'

The tour started with a ten-minute video on a big screen in a cinema-type room. It was all about the four finals each year, men's football, hurling, ladies' football and camogie – and had a behind-the-scenes look at what went on the day.

'Right, boys and girls,' the tour guide summoned them. 'It's time for our next stop on the tour, the changing rooms.'

The children gasped in disbelief as they walked into the changing rooms. County jerseys hung above every seat.

'Look how big it is in here,' Aidan gasped.

'It's about ten times the size of our changing rooms in Droichead,' John laughed.

'Look, lads, there's an indoor training area in here,' Aoife beckoned her friends.

Through a door at the side of the changing room was indeed a huge room with a high ceiling and Astro grass on the ground.

The tour guide explained that this is where the teams did the first part of their warm-ups on match days. He told the children that it would also be where team managers put motivational quotes on the walls and set up tactic boards.

From the dressing room in the Cusack Stand, the children then ran out, despite being told to walk, onto the grass of Croke Park, just like their county players would.

They stood excitedly at the side of the pitch.

'I wish I could kick a point here,' Billy whispered to Aoife.

'Me too,' Aoife hissed back. 'If I had a ball, I'd just run out there now and go for it.'

'You'd be thrown out,' Billy laughed.

'*Ciúnas*,' Ms Casey glared at them.

The tour guide explained about all the different areas of the stadium, showed them where the subs would sit, where the president would sit on All-Ireland finals day and where the television and radio commentary teams would be.

'Any questions?' he asked.

'How do they protect the grass when concerts are on here?' Tina asked. 'It looks so smooth; it must be awful to see it get ruined.'

'They have to replace most of it after each concert,' the guide told them. 'Steel coverings go down over it, and the grass dies underneath. The GAA have a special farm where they grow grass, and they bring it in specially after each concert and replace it. We have a brilliant team of grounds people,' he smiled.

'That's amazing,' Tina replied. 'I can't believe they replace it every time.'

'Yes, thankfully there aren't too many concerts on here,' the tour guide grinned.

The tour continued with the children visiting the corporate box level and then the top tier – where some people refused to go, as it was so steep and high.

'Ah c'mon, John,' Aidan tried to cajole his friend, 'come up here, look how amazing the views are.'

John stood stubbornly at the end of the stairs.

'I'm totally fine here, Aidan,' he shook his head.

'Suit yourself,' Aidan turned and looked again at the magnificent pitch. He closed his eyes, took a deep breath, and tried to picture himself playing there some day.

'Aidan, come on,' Ms Casey interrupted his thoughts. 'We're heading for the museum now.'

When the group arrived at the museum entrance, back near the shop at the start of the tour, the tour guide gathered everyone.

'I am going to leave you to explore the museum by yourselves now,' he announced. 'There are two levels. On the ground floor is the older history of the GAA, from the very start of its existence and covering the GAA during the War of Independence. There is a special Bloody Sunday exhibition here. There is the wall of fame for hurling and football. You will see the Sam Maguire and Liam McCarthy cups, behind glass of course,' he grinned.

'The upstairs is more modern history. You will find more about ladies' football here. Also, upstairs, we have lots of fun interactive games such as hit the button, fingertip save, knees up, high catch and many more. So have fun and I'll be nearby if you have any questions.'

'OK, boys and girls, off you go,' Ms Casey said. 'Stay in groups, no one by themselves and no messing.'

'I'm heading for the interactive games,' John said, heading toward the stairs.

'What about looking for information on the Lost Cup?' Sara asked. 'Oh, wow,' she said suddenly distracted, 'look at all the flags hanging from the ceiling.

'That's cool,' Billy replied, 'they are all the county flags.'

'Go to the games if you want,' Aidan said grumpily, 'I want to read the history stuff down here.'

'All right so,' John said, 'we'll all help you, Aidan, and then will we head for the games? Deal?'

'Deal!' Aidan said grinning. 'The games will be packed now anyway; everyone is gone up there. Look' it's nice and quiet down here,' he said pointing into the first part of the museum.

Aidan was right. It *was* quiet downstairs. It was dimly lit, so as to give a focus to the displays which were lit up and some parts had TV screens playing short informative films. A sense of calm descended as the gang walked in.

They all stopped and looked at a mannequin wearing replica camogie gear from the early 1900s, which included a full-length heavy black skirt and a white blouse buttoned up to the neck.

'How did they manage to play camogie wearing that?' Aoife asked incredulously.

'I don't know,' Tina replied. 'Look,' she continued laughing, 'It was a foul to stop the sliotar with your skirt!'

The girls burst into a fit of giggles as Aidan's eyes scanned the room for the War of Independence and Civil War sections.

Bingo, he thought as he saw a stand saying, 'The GAA and the struggle for Irish Independence'. He quickly read the paragraph about how the period from 1913 to 1923 was one of huge political transformation in Ireland and many GAA members featured in the developments at the time. This was, the paragraph said, a challenging time for the GAA. Aidan read more about the impact on the GAA of the Easter Rising in 1916 and of the atrocities of Bloody Sunday in November 1920 where fourteen

civilians were killed when British authorities opening fire in Croke Park itself. Aidan felt sick at the
thought of this. Young boys like himself had died
watching a match in the amazing stadium that he
was in.

Feeling quite emotional, Aidan read on about the
impact on the GAA of the treaty split that came after
the War of Independence. The treaty really divided
the Irish people, and GAA members were no different. It led to a Civil War between pro-treaty and
anti-treaty forces which wreaked havoc from April
1922 to May 1923. The Civil War divided families
and communities, especially in the south and west
of the country.

'That's our part of the country!' Aidan gasped.

Coming toward the end of the section now on
this period, Aidan wondered briefly where his
friends were before continuing to read about how
many GAA matches didn't go ahead during Civil
War times. But that when a truce was declared in
1923, how the GAA helped to bridge the divide
between pro- and anti-treaty supporters in its communities.

Aidan turned the corner to the last part of this section of the museum, disappointed that there was nothing about the Lost Cup, but stopped suddenly in his tracks.

'What's wrong?' he asked his friends.

Aoife, Billy, Sara, Tina, and John were standing, staring open-mouthed at the next display.

'What is it?' Aidan asked again.

'Aidan,' Aoife said, 'look.'

Aidan turned and looked to where Aoife was pointing, at a photo of a man, in his twenties, with dark brown hair. It was like looking in a mirror.

'Is that you, Aidan?' John laughed nervously. 'Did you go back in time or something?'

Aidan walked slowly toward the display captioned 'The GAA community during the Civil War'. Under the photo of the man who was the spitting image of Aidan, was a caption. It read:

'John Power, captain of the Coyle Gaels team, from Droichead Beag GAA, one of the greatest footballers of his time, and peacemaker during the Civil War. John Power is alleged to have hidden a cup that Coyle Gaels won, in what is now known as the mystery of the Lost Cup as it has never been found.'

'I don't believe it,' Aidan whispered to Aoife. 'Is he ... is he related to us?'

'It's fairly obvious that he is,' Aoife replied, just as Ms Casey arrived, telling them that time was up and to head back to the bus.

CHAPTER 14

The gang filed back on to the bus, still in shock. The minute Ms Casey was out of earshot, the whispering commenced.

'John Power was the captain of Coyle Gaels in November 1922. He *must* be related to you two,' Billy insisted. 'He is the spitting image of Aidan.'

'You mean Aidan is the spitting image of him,' John said.

'Whatever,' Billy said crossly, 'they *must* be related.'

'I agree,' Sara nodded.

'Look in the book Aidan,' Aoife urged. 'Have you read the chapters on the GAA during the Civil War yet?'

'No, good point, Aoife,' Aidan said, rushing

through unread chapters and opening Chapter 14, entitled 'Carrick, the GAA, and the Civil War'.

'Yes, look here, it's the same photo as in the museum,' Aidan said excitedly. 'I can't believe it was here all this time, right under my nose and I didn't see it.'

He read aloud.

'John Power was the captain of Coyle Gaels, a divisional team comprising of Carrick GAA, Droichead Beag GAA and Gorman GAA. He was born in 1900 on a farm in Droichead Beag, just outside the village and close to the banks of the River Coyle, which gave the divisional team its name. He was widely regarded as a magnificent Gaelic footballer and a born leader. It was no wonder that he was captain of the Coyle Gaels divisional team.

'Coyle Gaels won the county championship in November 1922, during the height of the Civil War. John Power was deeply troubled by the divisions in the population of the Carrick area caused by the pro- and anti-treaty split.

'The cup that was won by Coyle Gaels went missing in early 1923 and John Power would never talk about what happened to it. He would only confirm that it had been lost and said he hoped that it would no longer be seen as a divisive instrument and that the tension in the area due to different views on the treaty would start to heal.'

'Why was it divisive?' Billy asked.

'Good question, Billy,' Aoife replied. 'Could it be something to do with the war?'

Aidan kept reading.

'John married Peggy O'Mahony, and they ran a successful farm on his family land. John's grandson Joe still runs the farm today. Football runs in the family with Joe winning several county titles with Droichead Beag. His son Pat Power is the current minor captain of the club.'

'OMG,' Tina put her hand to her mouth. 'That's your dad – Pat Power.'

'When was this book written?' Aoife asked, 'it says he is a minor player.'

'It's old,' Aidan said, 'it was published in 1997, Dad would have been seventeen then; that makes sense.'

'So John Power is your great-great-grandfather, is that right?' John asked, counting on his fingers.

'It looks like it.' Aidan was pale. 'I can't believe it.'

'Wow,' Billy said. 'This is so cool. Your nana and grandad will surely be able to tell us where the Lost Cup is. John Power lived in their house. It's probably in the attic or something!'

'But why wouldn't they talk to us about it?' Aoife asked.

'Yeah, Aoife is right,' Aidan nodded. 'They are very cagey about it all, they don't want to talk about it.'

'It's not a very nice period in history for a lot of people,' John put in. 'The Civil War tore people apart. My dad often mentions it. Especially as it's the hundred-year anniversary of it right now.'

'Sorry, what's the treaty?' Sara asked quietly. 'I probably should know this.'

'No, in fairness, I don't think we have covered it in school yet,' Aidan said to Sara kindly. 'Your family came from Poland, and it wouldn't be common knowledge over there. It was the Anglo-Irish treaty. It was an agreement between Great Britain and Ireland to bring an end to the War of Independence. It meant that Ireland became a free state. Well, the twenty-six counties, not Northern Ireland. I think that Northern Ireland was created as part of the Treaty.'

'Why did some people not like it?' Sara asked.

'Because some people didn't think it went far enough,' Aidan explained. 'They wanted Ireland to be a full republic, with no links at all to Great Britain. Some people, like Michael Collins, who signed the treaty, wanted that too. But he felt that the violence in the War of Independence had to end and that he had to sign this treaty as it was the only offer on the table, and it would bring peace and an end to Irish people dying.'

'Did it bring peace?' Sara asked.

'Well, yes and no,' Aidan said. 'The Civil War started, which was between people who were for and against the treaty. Michael Collins was killed because of it. But then there was peace eventually.'

'But Ireland is a republic now?' Sara said.

'Yes, absolutely, officially since 1949,' Aidan said.

'I know where we are going first thing tomorrow morning,' Aoife said.

'To Nana and Grandad's house,' Aidan smiled. 'We won't be fobbed off this time.'

CHAPTER 15

The following morning was Saturday. Mr and Mrs Power looked up in surprise as Aoife and Aidan appeared down the stairs at 7.30am.

'I thought you two would be exhausted after your trip to Dublin,' Mr Power asked.

'Nope, lots to do today,' Aoife said.

'Busy day ahead,' Aidan added.

'What's going on?' their parents asked together.

'You two are up to something. I hope there is no more nonsense going on, playing tricks on Gorman kids,' their mam added warily.

'Don't worry, Mam,' Aoife laughed, 'that's not it. We're just calling up to see Nana and Grandad now.'

'Grandad won't be finished milking,' their dad said,

confused. 'It's not even 8am.'

'Actually, Dad, you might be able to help,' Aoife continued. 'Did you know your great-grandfather John Power was the captain of the Coyle Gaels divisional team that won the county championship in 1922 and hid the Lost Cup afterwards?'

'*Allegedly* hid,' Aidan added.

'Woah, there's a lot of statements and questions rolled into one,' Mr Power said looking even more confused. 'Yes, John Power was my great-grandfather, I remember him.'

'You do?' Aidan was incredulous. 'He must have been ancient if you remember him.'

'He never seemed ancient, Aidan. He lived to be ninety, he died in 1990 I think. I would have been nearly finished primary school when he passed away. I remember him all through my childhood. He was strong as an ox; he was always kicking ball with myself and my brothers and sisters.'

Excitement was leaping out of Aoife and Aidan.

'Did he tell you where he hid the Lost Cup, Dad, please tell me he did?' Aidan almost shouted.

'Calm down, you two,' Mrs Power said, 'Where did

you hear all this?'

'His photo is in the Croke Park museum, Mam,' Aoife said. 'He's famous.'

'I don't know about that,' Mr Power continued. 'I mean, he was a great footballer, and I knew he was captain and that he won titles with Droichead and with Coyle Gaels, but I don't know anything about the Lost Cup. Is he really in the Croke Park museum?' Mr Power shook his head in disbelief.

'You don't remember anything?' Aidan slouched in disappointment.

'No, I mean I've heard the rumours about it being lost or hidden, but I really don't think it was Grandad John, as we called him, that was involved.'

'Dad,' Aoife said slowly, 'I think you might be wrong. Show him, Aidan.'

Aidan carefully opened the history book that Ms Casey had given to him and showed his parents the paragraph about John Power.

'Look at that,' Mr Power exclaimed. 'Now how come my parents haven't told me about this?'

'How come indeed!' Aidan said triumphantly. 'Now you know why we want to talk to them.'

'I'm coming with you,' Mr Power said, quickly lacing up his runners.

'Clare is still asleep,' their mam said. 'I'll stay here until she wakes up and follow you up.'

Mr Power, Aoife, and Aidan ran across the shortcut through the fields at the back of Amber Fields that brought them to the Powers' farmhouse.

Joe, the twins' grandad, was coming out of the milking parlour as they arrived, his morning work just finished.

'What's wrong?' were the first words out of his mouth when he saw his son and two grandchildren moving towards him at speed at 8am.

'Nothing's wrong,' Mr Power laughed. 'The twins and I just want to ask you about something.'

'At this hour,' Joe laughed. 'Pity you didn't come an hour earlier, and you could have helped with the milking.'

A few minutes later, the twins, their dad, Joe and Mary sat themselves down at the sturdy farmhouse kitchen table, with mugs of tea and buttery toast in front of them.

'Well now, what do you want to ask me about this

early in the morning?' Joe said as he took a long sup of tea.

'The Lost Cup,' Aidan grinned.

'Not this again, Aidan pet,' Mary exclaimed.

'Nana, we have more information now,' Aoife smiled.

The twins relayed their story of the Croke Park museum and the local history book, which they showed to their nana and grandad.

'Is it true, did John Power really hide the cup?' Aidan asked eagerly.

'Do you know where it is, Grandad? Imagine if we found it,' Aoife said excitedly, 'RTÉ would probably come and film us.'

'There'll be no RTÉ,' Joe said sternly. 'My grand-father would not have wanted any attention brought to this cup.'

'You do know about it?' Aoife asked slowly.

'I do,' Joe sighed. 'Well, I don't know where it is, but I know why he hid it.'

Aidan gasped. 'So, he did hide it!'

'Aidan, if I tell you this story, you are going to have to calm down,' Joe said seriously. 'This is not a funny story; it hasn't been spoken about for a long time.'

'I can't believe this!' Mr Power said. 'I never knew my great-grandfather was the person who hid the Lost Cup. 'Why didn't you tell me, Dad?'

'You never asked, Pat,' Mary interrupted. 'Some things are best left unspoken. I don't know if this is a good idea, Joe,' she frowned.

'Mary, they've read what's in that history book. I don't know a whole lot more, but I will tell them what I know. It's a wonder more people haven't asked about it before. That book is out there in public view. I don't think many people bother reading about history around here anymore though. Matt Kelly, he knows the story.'

'Is that Matt, the history guy we met at the kiln?' Aoife asked.

'Yes, that's him. He wrote this book, Aoife.'

'What?' Aoife and Aidan looked at the cover. How had they missed that?

'As you have read,' Joe started, 'my grandfather John Power was the captain of Coyle Gaels, and he was a magnificent footballer. Strong as an ox. Coyle Gaels won the county championship in November

1922, during the height of the Civil War. Grandad John was a republican, like most people were, but he was not a violent man. He had learned to live with the violence during the War of Independence as he felt that there was no choice, but he couldn't countenance Irish people fighting Irish people in the Civil War. It felt so wrong to him.

'You must remember, Aoife and Aidan, that this was a very tense and troubled time in Irish history, when friends and neighbours who were for or against the treaty turned on each other. It saddened my grandfather to see this in the country and especially in the parish that he loved.

'Not long after the Cup was won by Coyle Gaels, the Civil War came to a peak in our area. Some of my grandfather's teammates on the Coyle Gaels team fell out. A lot of the Gorman side were pro-treaty whereas a lot of the Droichead side were anti-treaty. Carrick were a mixed bag.

'One night, my grandfather and some of his friends and teammates from Droichead, including William Donovan, were here at this table playing cards. There was a knock at the door and some of their Coyle

Gaels teammates from Gorman were outside. The Gorman men were on a mission, they said they had come to take the cup, as they didn't want it in the hands of anti-treaty men. William Donovan was a notorious republican, and it was probably the fact that he was present and so friendly with John Power that really riled them up. My grandfather told them to go home to their beds and that they would talk about it in the morning when they had all calmed down, and come to an arrangement about the Cup. But one of the Gorman men drew a gun. He aimed it at William Donovan. My grandfather made a dive for him and managed to divert the trajectory of the bullet. It hit William Donovan in the leg, instead of the chest. The Gorman men panicked and fled.

'Truth be told, this was probably less about politics and the treaty and more about rivalries in the Coyle Gaels team between Droichead and Gorman play-ers, the same old rubbish that still goes on today. But with no guns, thankfully, now.' He shook his head sadly.

'After that, my grandfather hid the cup, in the hope that it would put an end to fighting between the villages. The Gorman men were spooked after what happened to William Donovan so there was no more talk about it. They weren't big fighters either, they just made a stupid decision that night. That's it, really, no more to tell.'

'What happened William Donovan?' Mr Power asked.

'He lost his leg,' Joe said solemnly. 'He could never play football again of course and he struggled to find work. It made for a hard time for the Donovans.'

'Is that Billy's great-great-grandfather?' Aidan asked slowly.

Joe nodded.

'Does Billy know?' Aoife asked.

'Oh, I doubt it,' Joe replied. 'His grandfather, my friend, died young, God rest him, and I'd say Billy's dad has no idea.'

'So, you don't know where the Cup is?' Aidan asked sadly

'I have no idea, I swear,' Joe replied. 'More to the point, I don't want you two to go looking for it.'

'Why not, Grandad?' Aoife moaned.

'Haven't you listened to a word I said, young lady?

It's bad news.'

'That was a hundred years ago, Grandad,' Aoife insisted. 'There's no Civil War now.'

'Yeah, wouldn't it be great to find a bit of our history,' Aidan smiled.

'I give up.' Joe threw his hands in the air, exasperated. 'I don't know did you listen to me at all. But sure, it's all the one. My grandfather was a clever man. No one has found the Cup in a hundred years; I don't think you two will find it now.'

Aoife looked slowly at Aidan, who was smirking at her.

Oh no, their dad thought to himself. *They won't rest until it's found.*

CHAPTER 16

By lunchtime on Saturday, Aidan had gathered what he called an emergency meeting of the Amber Fields Gang. That of course included John who was back cycling now and had made his way as fast as possible to Amber Fields when he heard that there was news on the Lost Cup.

At two o'clock, Aoife, Aidan, and Sara were sitting on the bench at the side of the green in Amber Fields. John and Tina were sitting on the ground in front of them. Max, Tina's dog was in between them. Max was enjoying getting belly rubs from Tina and John alternatively.

'C'mon, Aidan,' John moaned, 'tell us what you found out.'

'No, we have to wait for Billy,' Aidan said seriously.

Five minutes later, Billy ran toward the gang, football in hand, soloing as he moved.

'The skills competition is tomorrow,' he explained, 'I have to keep practising.'

'You can put the ball down for five minutes Billy,' John said with a wave of his hand. 'You'll be grand, you're bound to win.'

'I don't think so, John,' Billy replied. 'There's a load of good players from all over the county coming to this.'

'We'll be there to support you all the way,' Aoife smiled.

Billy looked up surprised, then blushed bright red and looked away. Tina and Sara exchanged a glance as Aidan launched into his story about the Lost Cup, oblivious to anything else happening.

When Aidan had recounted the story that the twins' grandparents had told them about the Lost Cup, there was a stunned silence in the group. Billy was the first one to break it.

'So, you're saying that my great-great-grandfather lost his leg during an argument about a football cup during the Civil War?' he asked incredulously.

'That's what Grandad Joe said,' Aoife confirmed sadly.

'How come my dad never told me any of this?' Billy asked.

'Maybe he doesn't know,' Aidan suggested. 'Grandad Joe said that your grandad died quite young – he was friends with our grandad – so maybe your dad was never told.'

'Maybe,' Billy said shaking his head. 'That's so weird.'

'What does this all mean for the Lost Cup?' Tina asked.

'I think it means we leave well enough alone,' John grunted.

'What do you mean, John?' Sara asked.

'It's obviously bad news,' John replied. 'Civil War times were horrible in Ireland, Sara, by all accounts. People turned on each other. I mean, even Michael Collins was killed, and no one ever thought that would happen, and in his own county and all. Now we hear that Gorman and Droichead people fought over this Lost Cup, but really fought over sides in the

Civil War and that Billy's great-great-grandfather lost his leg! I say we should forget about the Lost Cup, it's bad news. Your great-great-grandfather hid it for a good reason, Aidan. It caused trouble. Leave it be.'

'Yeah, it could be cursed!' Sara added dramatically.

'No,' Aidan said stubbornly. 'This is a part of our history, John; we need to find it. All that fighting was a hundred years ago, there's no Civil War anymore.'

'There's still fighting now,' John snorted. 'Look at yourself and Tommy Doyle.'

'It's not just *me* and Tommy Doyle,' Aidan retaliated. 'None of us like him. But that's totally different John. We don't go around shooting people.'

'No, just putting yoghurt in their shoes,' Aoife grinned, thinking back to their tit-for-tat incidents with Gorman the previous year.

Billy laughed. 'Ah, John, you're taking this too seriously, I reckon. What harm can it do to look for the cup? And if we find it, we'll be famous.'

'Thanks, Billy,' Aidan smiled.

As John stood up huffing about them being as mad as their ancestors, Aoife smiled to herself and thought that maybe, the Lost Cup that had been so divisive a hundred years ago, could bring their group – and especially Billy and Aidan – back together now.

***

Hours later, the six of them sat tired and disillusioned outside the milking parlour on the Power farm.

'This is impossible,' John moaned, 'you know that, Aidan, impossible. We've searched every outhouse in this farm and nothing. That's before you even start on the fields.'

'Who's to say that he even hid it on his own farm?' Tina added, siding firmly with John. 'He could have hidden it anywhere in Droichead. He could even have hidden it in Gorman. Maybe Tommy Doyle is right.'

'Tommy Doyle is never right, Tina,' Billy said firmly. 'I'm sorry, Aidan,' he said, 'but do you mind if I call it a night? I have the skills competition tomorrow.'

'That's fine, Billy,' Aoife spoke for Aidan who had his head buried in an old Ordnance Survey map that he had found at home. 'We're heading home soon anyway.'

'Sorry, what?' Aidan said looking up distractedly. 'Go home, let you all go away if you want, I've a load more ideas of where to search.'

'Look, Aoife,' he said excitedly to his twin, as Billy, John, Tina, and Sara headed for home, 'look here on the map.'

Aoife squinted. 'Is that a well?' she asked.

'Yes,' Aidan said excitedly, 'in the back field, that must be it. It's old, so it would have been here a hundred years ago.'

'OK, Aidan,' Aoife nodded. 'In in the morning, right?' she continued firmly. 'It's getting dark, and I don't want to fall into a well. Or have you fall into a well,' she nudged her brother. 'C'mon, let's get home. We can come back tomorrow better prepared, with a shovel maybe, and Dad's big torch.'

'All right,' Aidan agreed. 'The minute Billy's competition is over, we're going there, OK?'

'OK,' Aoife agreed.

CHAPTER 17

Aoife, Aidan, Tina, and Sara hopped out of Mr Power's car at Carrick pitch the following morning. Crowds were milling around, and excitement was building for the county skills competition.

They quickly found a good spot in the stand from where to watch Billy and Darragh compete. John scurried in with seconds to go just as the first round was about to start.

'Have I missed anything?' he hissed.

No, you're just in time,' Sara grinned. 'I can't wait for this, I'm so excited.'

'Me too,' Tina added, 'I really hope Billy wins.'

'What do you have there, Aidan?' John asked, noticing Aidan with his head in a book.

'It's just the history book. I was reading more about the Lost Cup,' Aidan replied.

'Obsessed,' John mouthed to Tina and Sara.

'Cop on, John,' Aoife said crossly, coming to her brother's defence.

'Someone's in a mood,' John smirked at Aoife.

'Shh! It's starting,' Aoife hushed him.

'Shh, John!' taunted Tommy Doyle appearing seemingly from thin air behind them. 'Don't you know she needs to concentrate on watching her boyfriend.'

'Shut up, Tommy!' Aoife shouted. 'I've had enough of your smart comments. Billy is my *friend*. Isn't Ellie always next to you, maybe I should start saying that she's *your* girlfriend.'

'Oooh, someone got out the wrong side of bed this morning,' Tommy laughed. 'All right, Aoife, you've made your point. Let's call it quits and watch the lads.'

'Wow,' Tina whispered to Aoife when Tommy was out of earshot. 'He totally changed his tune when you stood up to him.'

'I'm shaking a small bit,' Aoife admitted. 'But it

did feel good!'

The noise in the crowd died down suddenly and Aoife focused her attention on watching Darragh and Billy in the first skills test, which was free kicks. They could kick the ball off the ground or from the hand from the 20-metre line. They had to kick three times from each leg.

'Billy is ambidextrous, he'll be flying it here,' John said confidently.

'What did you say?' Tina asked him. 'Doesn't ambidextrous mean you can use both hands equally? You mean Billy can kick off both legs equally?'

'Yeah, smarty pants,' John said crossly. 'It also means you can use both *legs* equally. My aunt is an occupational therapist and she told me!'

'Wasn't I right,' he said triumphantly as Billy successfully kicked six free kicks over the bar, three from his left foot and three from his right.

'Alright, John,' Tina smiled. 'You were right,'

'We'll give you this one, John,' Aoife laughed.

'See, I can surprise you all sometimes with my amazing general knowledge,' John retorted.

Aoife looked over at Aidan who was unusually

quiet. Instead of being engrossed in watching the skills competition, as Aoife thought he would be, he was engrossed in the history book.

'Look, Aoif,' he hissed, 'look at the photo of the Carrick team that John Power was captain of. Look at the names, William Donovan (Droichead Beag), he's Billy relative, David Tracey (Droichead Beag), he must be related to John, and look at this, Thomas Doyle (Gorman).'

'Tommy's relation?' Aoife asked.

'Must be,' Aidan said seriously. 'Grandad Joe said that most Gorman men were pro-treaty and that they were the ones who called to the house with the gun. What if it was Thomas Doyle that shot Billy's great-great-grandfather?'

'Ah, Aidan, calm down,' Aoife said looking at the urgent expression on her brother's face. 'You don't know that at all.'

'I *have* to find the cup, Aoife,' Aidan said desperately.

'Why, Aidan?' Aoife asked kindly. 'I know it would be cool to find it, but you don't have to. Maybe we should take a break from looking for it. We need to be training for the championship, our chance to beat

Gorman, we can focus on that. It's my last competition ever playing for Droichead GAA. I can't play with the boys anymore after this year.'

'I know,' Aidan said sadly. 'I really want to find it, though.'

'You are getting a bit obsessed,' Aoife said.

'It's my chance to fix things, to do something right,' Aidan burst out.

'What do you mean?' Aoife asked.'

'I messed up in the skills competition,' Aidan said sadly, 'then I played terrible in the league final and cost us the match, now Billy doesn't want to be friends with me anymore. At least if I find the cup, I'll have succeeded at something.'

'Aidan, sorry but that's a load of rubbish,' Aoife said sternly to her brother. 'Billy is still your friend and, yeah, you weren't at your best in the final, but everyone has an off day. We'll have plenty more days to play Gorman again. You need to calm down.'

Aidan looked upset. 'I'm going to the shop,' he sulked and stood up and walked off.

'Is Aidan going to the shop?' John looked up absentmindedly. 'Aidan, get me a can of coke, will you?'

But Aidan didn't even look back.

Five rounds later, and after a masterclass in soloing, kicking, and handpassing, Billy was the overwhelming winner.

'I can't believe that our Billy is county skills champion,' John said. 'I've a tear in my eye.'

'Ah John, that's so sweet,' Aoife said, shouldering John gently.

A little while later, after he'd had his photo taken and his hand shaken what felt like a few hundred times, Billy made his way towards them with his trophy.

'Well done, Billy!' Sara and Tina squealed.

Tommy and Ellie came over and patted Billy on the back.

'Fair play, you deserved that, boy,' Tommy said grudgingly.

'Didn't he?' Darragh grinned as he joined them. 'No one near him in terms of skills, amazing stuff.'

'Well done, Billy,' Aoife said suddenly shy, for some reason unknown to her.

'Thanks, Aoife,' Billy said quietly. 'Where's Aidan?'

'He's at the shop,' Aoife said. 'Although, wait, that was ages ago. Did he come back, John?'

'No,' John confirmed.

'You lost track of your brother; you were so into the skills competition,' Darragh laughed.

'Dad, where's Aidan?' Aoife shouted at her father, who was a few rows in front of them.

'He went home with Mam,' Mr Power shouted back. 'Clare wasn't feeling well, and Aidan said he had something to do, so Mam took them home. We'll go home with Billy's mam and dad shortly.'

'Oh,' Aoife said.

'Right,' Billy said, deflated. 'He didn't see me win so.'

'Mustn't have,' Aoife agreed sadly.

'Anyway,' Tina said, trying to cover up the awkwardness, 'aren't we going to check out that well when we get back?'

'Oh yeah,' Sara said excitedly, 'imagine if the Cup was there!'

'Do ye know where the Cup is?' Darragh asked interested.

'Em, no,' Aoife replied. 'Aidan has an idea, but it's

probably wrong.'

'Is that where he's gone?' Billy asked.

'Ah no, he'd have waited for us surely,' John said.

'Well, this is going to be great fun,' Tommy said loudly. 'A great big gang of us, all heading to Droichead to find the Lost Cup. C'mon Aoife, lead the way – this is going to be good.'

CHAPTER 18

'**W**hy did they all have to come as well?' John muttered under his breath, turning his head in the direction of Tommy Doyle, as he climbed out of Billy's dad's seven-seater car in Amber Fields.

Aoife and Billy hopped out of the back seat behind him and quickly set off in the direction of the Power's farm.

'Hey, wait up,' Tommy shouted, as he got out of Maeve's mam's car with Darragh, Ellie and Maeve. 'Wait for us, we can't wait to see this famous Lost Cup. I hope Aidan hasn't hidden it again by the time we get there,' he guffawed.

'Where are you all off to?' Mr Power asked suspiciously, seeing the larger than usual gang, including four kids from Gorman.

'Erm, I think Aidan is gone up to Nana and Grandad's, we're just going up to meet him there,' Aoife said quickly.

'That's right,' Mrs Power said, sticking her head out of the door of the Powers' house. 'Aidan headed off the minute we got home, he said he wanted to talk to Nana and Grandad again about this Lost Cup.'

'But why are you all going up there?' Mr Power tried again, still confused.

'Oh, we want to see this new river walk thing Mr Power,' Darragh said quickly. 'Billy said it's really cool and that you can get to it on the other side of the farm, is that right?' he asked innocently.

Billy smiled at Mr Power in what he hoped was a convincing manner.

'Yeah, that's right,' Mr Power said. 'Right, don't be long, Aoife. Dinner will be ready soon. Bring Aidan home with you.'

'OK, Dad,' Aoife smiled.

The big gang headed off in the direction of the Powers' farm.

Tina and Sara joined them as they walked out the back of Amber Fields and onto the Powers' farmland.

'Well, this is gas,' Darragh said trying to lighten the mood, 'all of us together looking for the Lost Cup.'

'Setting our differences aside,' Tommy smirked. 'I can't wait.'

'Where is this well at all, Aoife?' Maeve asked kindly.

'I'm not sure,' Aoife muttered. 'Aidan said it was in the top field, but that's all I know.'

'We'll find it,' Billy reassured her.

'Aidan would surely have found it by now?' Tina questioned. 'He left Carrick ages ago.'

'He's probably sitting in your grandparent's farmhouse eating biscuits by now,' John laughed. 'Examining the Lost Cup!'

'Let's check, it's on the way,' Aoife said.

A few minutes later, she reappeared on the porch of her grandparents' house, a worried look on her face.

'He's not here,' she whispered to Billy. 'I didn't say anything to Nana and Grandad about the well as I didn't want to worry them. I have a bad feeling.'

'Bad twin feeling?' Billy asked.

Aoife nodded.

'Why did he go looking for an old well all by him-self?' she groaned. 'He should have waited for us. The well is dry though, at least as far as I know. I just still have this bad feeling.'

'Let's go, quickly,' Billy urged.

'C'mon,' Ellie moaned, 'this is boring. There's no way that Aidan found that Lost Cup.'

'But what if he did, Ellie? Darragh said encourag-ingly. 'How cool would that be?'

Five minutes later they entered the top field.

'Where would a well be?' Billy asked.

John quickly scanned the field.

'Might be near that old mound of stones,' he said. 'I know there is a well like that on our land.'

They hurried towards the stones, Aoife's bad feel-ing increasing with every step.

'Aidan,' she called out urgently, 'are you here, Aidan?'

No response.

They reached the mound of old grey stones and there was no sign of a well. Tommy's eyes scanned the ground.

'No well here,' Sara said brightly, 'it must be somewhere else, Aoife.'

'What are you on about?' Tommy said, 'it's probably here all right. Just keep looking.'

'What do you mean? Sara asked, 'there is no little circular stone thing with a bucket hanging off it.'

'Ah stop,' Tommy laughed. 'You're thinking of fairy tales. A well here could be just a hole in the ground. These stones could have been built around it years ago.'

'Oops, sorry!' Sara laughed.

'Actually, be careful,' Tommy cautioned, 'you might not notice the hole, this place is very overgrown.'

'Here,' Billy called out suddenly, 'look, the briars have been moved.'

'Careful now,' Tommy cautioned.

Tommy, Billy, and Aoife inched forward slowly, pulled back the briars and to their horror, at the bottom of what looked like a five-metre hole in the ground, lay Aidan and he wasn't moving.

CHAPTER 19

'AIDAN!' Aoife roared.

'Aidan, up here,' Billy shouted behind her.

'Oh no,' Tommy's face was white.

Then, to Aoife's intense relief, Aidan looked up and croaked 'Aoife, Billy, Tommy?'

'Are you all right?' Aoife shouted, 'what happened?'

'I hurt my ankle,' Aidan said slowly, 'I think I sprained it. I climbed down, but I slipped, the rocks are greasy, and when I fell, I banged my ankle. Now I can't move.'

'We have to get him out,' Billy said urgently.

'We need a rope,' Tommy said.

'I'll run back to the farm and get one,' said Billy.

'I'll come with you,' John said, 'I have an idea

158

where they would keep them.'

As John and Billy ran off, Aoife looked worriedly down at her brother.

'Are you OK?' she shouted.

'I'm a bit cold.' Aidan said, 'and I don't like the dark, but it's better now that you gang are here. Em, why are you here, Tommy?'

'We thought you'd find the Lost Cup,' Tommy laughed. 'We wanted to make sure that we were here to see that. I take it it's not down there?'

'No, it's not,' Aidan said sadly. 'I have checked. I've had a bit of time,' he added wryly.

'Do you know what?' Tommy said suddenly, 'I reckon I could climb down far enough to help get him out.'

'Don't be stupid, Tommy,' Ellie said, 'You'll just get stuck as well.'

'No, I'm a lot taller than you all,' Tommy said. 'If I can get down far enough, I can stick out my hand and pull him up.'

'This is madness,' Aoife said.

'For once I agree with you, Aoife,' Ellie sniffed.

Tommy had already sat down at the top of the

opening and had swung his long legs around and was climbing down slowly using some makeshift footholds on the side of the well.

'Can you stand, Aidan?' he shouted. 'I should have asked you that before I started coming down here.'

'Yeah, I can put weight on the other foot,' Aidan confirmed. 'Hang on.'

He slowly stood up using the sides of the well as support.

'I can put a little weight on the bad foot actually,' he said brightly. 'This might not be as bad as I thought.'

'Pity,' Tommy laughed. 'I thought you might be out of action for the championship.'

'Ah, Tommy, just pull him out,' Darragh said urgently.

'All right, keep your hair on, I'm only joking,' Tommy laughed.

Tommy carefully stretched out his arm and Aidan, not quite believing that his sworn enemy, Tommy Doyle from Gorman, was helping him, grabbed it quickly.

'Now we'll climb back up together,' Tommy

ordered. 'You use your good foot and lean on me on your left-hand side with the bad foot.'

Moments later, Billy and John arrived back at the well, a rope in their hands and stood open-mouthed at the sight of Tommy Doyle pulling Aidan Power out of the well.

Darragh grinned and nudged Billy. 'I told you he wasn't all bad,' he whispered.

'I didn't believe you until this moment,' Billy said shocked.

'Right, c'mon, Darragh, I'm off,' Tommy said suddenly. 'I've had enough of Droichead now, no Lost Cup. It's getting boring.'

'Thanks, Tommy,' Aidan said quietly.

'Yeah, thanks so much for helping,' Aoife said.

'No bods,' Tommy grinned, 'you can repay me by losing in the championship and letting us do the double.'

'Ah, I can't promise that' Aidan laughed. 'I do owe you one, though.'

'Good luck,' Tommy said, turned on his heel and was gone.

'Right see you,' Maeve waved as she, Ellie and

Darragh headed for home also.

'Wow,' John said, 'just wow.'

'I don't know what to say,' Tina said, open-mouthed.

'Does this mean there is a truce?' Sara asked.

'This is new territory, Sara,' Aidan said solemnly, 'I just don't know.'

The calmness was broken by the sound of the twins' grandmother, rushing towards them shouting.

'What's going on? Who's hurt?' she said loudly arriving next to them. 'I saw the boys looking for a rope and I said what in blazes' name are they up to.'

'I got stuck in the well, Nana,' Aidan said softly.

'What were you doing in there?' Mary shouted.

'Looking for the Lost Cup,' Aidan said sheepishly.

'Aidan,' Mary said, exasperatedly. 'You've got to forget this nonsense. Now, look at you, a sore foot and you're lucky to be alive.'

'Ah Nana, he's not that bad,' Aoife started.

'Aoife, he nearly put the heart crossways on me,' Mary cautioned her granddaughter. 'What were that gang from Gorman doing here?' she eyed them all suspiciously. 'I hope there was no high jinks or messing going on here.'

'No, Nana, they were just excited to see the Lost Cup,' Aoife explained. 'Tommy Doyle even helped Aidan out of the well.'

'Maybe he isn't the worst,' Aidan admitted, 'even if his ancestors were involved in shooting William Donovan.'

'What are you talking about, Aidan?' Mary asked crossly. 'I thought Grandad explained all that to you. Whoever let off that gun, it certainly wasn't Thomas Doyle. He was friends with John Power. Thomas Doyle was trying to keep the peace that night between the Droichead men and the Gorman men.'

'He was?' Aidan asked incredulously.

'Yes, he was,' Mary said gruffly. 'Don't always judge a book by its cover, Aidan. The Doyles might be tough, and I know you have had your differences with Tommy, but they are not all bad. Not everything is black and white, my boy. Now off home with you all. And don't let me catch any of you near that well again.'

Mary turned for home, muttering about blocking off the well properly.

'I suppose that's it so,' John said breaking the silence.

'Yeah,' Aidan said quietly. 'I reckon the search for the Lost Cup is over. Sorry, guys,' he continued, trying to get up from where he was sitting on the grass. 'I got a bit obsessed with it. I haven't been much fun recently.'

'Don't worry about it, buddy,' John said lightly.

'No, it's not right,' Aidan said. 'I left Billy's skills competition; I can't believe I did that.'

'It's OK, Aidan,' Billy said graciously.

'No, it's not,' Aidan continued. 'I'm guessing you won?'

'Yeah,' Billy said shyly.

'By a mile,' Sara added.

'I should have been there,' Aidan groaned. 'I was just *so* convinced that the Cup was in the well, and then I was looking at Tommy Doyle and thinking that his ancestor Thomas had shot William Donovan. I just had to go and try and solve it and find the Lost Cup. Turns out I was wrong on both counts, wrong about Thomas Doyle and wrong about the Lost Cup.'

'You usually are right,' Tina said smiling, 'it must be strange to be wrong! But it happens to all of us,

Aidan.'

Aidan gave a small smile.

'I've just been so stupid,' he said. 'I haven't been thinking straight. I kept thinking that our gang was breaking up, that Billy would be friends with Darragh and the Gorman gang and forget about us, and that Tina was giving up football and wouldn't play with us anymore. I thought if I found the Lost Cup, that it would bring us all back together. It was so silly.'

'It wasn't totally stupid,' John said. 'I mean, it did bring us all together and it even brought us together with the Gorman gang. Maybe they aren't so bad. But going into the well yourself, yeah, that was stupid.' He laughed.

'This gang isn't going anywhere, Aidan,' Billy said suddenly. 'Yeah, I'm friends with Darragh, but sure we all are. And Maeve. And now it turns out that Tommy might be all right at times.'

'Thanks, Bill,' Aidan said quietly. 'So, we're OK?'

'We're OK,' Billy nodded smiling.

'I'm not going anywhere either,' Tina said loudly.

'I know, Tina,' Aidan replied. 'You're back playing

football with the girls. That's great.'

'I might do one better than that,' Tina smiled. 'I've been thinking, the championship is our very last competition with Droichead, us girls that is, so wouldn't I be mad to miss it?'

'Seriously?' Aoife asked.

Tina nodded.

'That's unreal news,' Aoife shouted, hugging Tina.

'That's class,' Billy added, 'we have our full back back!'

'Too many backs in that sentence,' John laughed.

'C'mon,' Billy said putting his hand out to Aidan.

Aidan grabbed it and started walking gingerly.

'This mightn't be too bad,' he said again, smiling.

The six of them headed back slowly towards Amber Fields.

'Championship, here we come,' John shouted, jumping in the air.

CHAPTER 20

Six weeks passed and summer was ending. A sense of calm had descended on the Amber Fields gang.

Matches had resumed in the green, with the six of Aidan, Aoife, Billy, Tina, Sara and John. Sometimes their siblings joined in, sometimes some of the Gorman gang called over, mainly Darragh and Maeve, but sometimes Tommy. Never Ellie. Tommy was still a pain at times, but something had changed this summer. Had they changed or had Tommy changed? Maybe they were just all growing up. It was good as they would be going to secondary school with the Gorman kids next month, so it was better that everyone got along.

The under-12 county championship had started a few weeks ago. Tina stayed true to her word and came back playing for Droichead. The team were playing well together and as many had predicted, they won their first-round match, then their quarter- and semi-final. Also, as many had predicted, Gorman did the same on the other side of the draw. This was no surprise, considering they had been the top two teams in the league back in the spring.

The scene was set for a rematch with the final a week away, at the end of August, and Droichead had a point to prove, having lost the league final. *Things feel different now,* Aidan thought to himself as he kicked a ball off the side of the Powers' house on a Sunday evening. Back in the spring, the gang had felt disjointed. Now they felt like a strong unit again. Training was fun, everyone was in good form. John was back from injury; Tina was back playing. It was sad to think that the girls only had one more match playing for Droichead Beag GAA.

This is getting boring by myself, Aidan thought and ball in hand, headed inside and upstairs to see what Aoife was doing.

'What's up, Aoif?' He casually threw himself down on a chair in Aoife's room.

'Nothing much,' Aoife replied. 'I'm just putting the finishing touches to my painting.'

'What are you painting now?' Aidan asked.

Aoife always had some painting on the go. There were specks of paint all over her desk and the floor near it, which Mam and Dad were always giving out about.

'I need an artist's studio in the back garden,' Aoife was fond of telling them.

'It's the lime kiln on the greenway,' Aoife replied. 'Remember I started sketching it back at the start of the summer? I went down and took some more photos there recently. They have almost finished restoring it, it's so cool. I'm nearly finished my painting.'

'Show me,' Aidan said absentmindedly.

'You'll have to come here,' Aoife said, 'It's still wet.'

Aidan shrugged and slowly got up from the chair, yawning.

'Wow, that's actually really good,' Aidan commented, noticing the vivid colours and detail that

Aoife had put into the stonework. Something niggled at him as he looked at the painting.

'Don't sound so surprised,' Aoife nudged her twin good-naturedly.

'Ah no, I don't mean it like that,' Aidan said, flopping down on Aoife's bed. 'I'm so tired,' he yawned again.

'Hey, get off that,' Aoife said, 'I have photos there.'

'Oops, sorry,' Aidan said, pulling a pile of photos out from beneath where he had thrown himself. 'What are these? he asked. 'Oh, they are your photos of the lime kiln?'

'Uh huh,' Aoife confirmed, working away diligently on her painting.

'What's that house in the background?' Aidan asked suddenly. 'It looks familiar.'

'That Nana and Grandad's house, silly,' Aoife said. 'The greenway is at the back of their farm. Remember Matt, the historian, was telling us about the lime kiln, the day we were kicking around in the clearing? I met him last week and he was saying that he had found out since that the lime kiln *did* belong to the Powers. When he was talking to us that day, he wasn't sure.'

Aidan went quiet.

'Aoife, when did Matt say that farmers stopped using lime kilns?' he asked slowly, after a moment.

'Oh, he just told me this the last day,' Aoife said brightly, happy to pass on interesting information to her brother. 'He said that around a hundred years ago, farmers stopped using lime kilns on their land as there were bigger commercial lime kilns built where you could just buy lime. It was cheaper and easier to buy it than having to use their own lime kilns.'

Aidan stood up quickly and looked at Aoife's painting again. Then he looked at the photo in his hand, and back at the painting.

'Aidan, what's wrong?' Aoife asked. 'Why are you so quiet?'

Aidan kept staring.

'Aidan,' Aoife asked again, 'what's going on?'

'Aoife,' Aidan said finally, 'that's where it is.'

'Where what is?' Aoife said exasperatedly, but as the words left her mouth, she knew.

'The Lost Cup,' they both said together.

'I'll get my bike,' Aidan said quickly. 'You get Billy,

Tina and Sara and follow on. I'll ring John.'

'Aidan, stop,' Aoife said, 'we are all going together. Remember the well, you are not going alone. We will get everyone and go together.'

Aidan looked like he was about to bolt, but then he stood at the top of the stairs and nodded.

'Actually,' he said thoughtfully, 'will you ring Maeve and tell her to bring the Gorman gang too if they want to come? To be fair, I owe Tommy one, and I know he really wants to see the Lost Cup.'

'Are you really sure it's in there?' Aoife asked.

'As sure as I can be,' Aidan replied. 'It makes so much sense. If I'm wrong, I promise, I will give up on this once and for all.'

An hour later, the six from the Amber Fields gang plus the Gorman four of Darragh, Maeve, Tommy and Ellie were standing in front of the lime kiln.

'I can't believe that everyone got here so quickly,' Aoife laughed.

'This IS the moment we've been waiting for,' John

said excitedly.

'You'd better not be wasting our time,' Ellie growled.

'Give it a rest, Ellie,' Darragh said.

'What makes you so sure, out of interest?' Tommy asked.

'We've just found out that this lime kiln belonged to our ancestors, it was on the Power farm,' Aidan began.

'A historian told us this,' Aoife added. 'He also told us that lime kilns stopped being used around a hundred years ago, because there were bigger commercial kilns that it was easier to get lime from.'

'It was a hundred years ago that Coyle Gaels won the Lost Cup,' Billy said slowly.

'Yes,' Aidan nodded.

'John Power would have been farming here back then?' John asked.

'Yes, again,' Aidan confirmed.

'I see your reasoning,' Sara smiled.

'Let's see the proof so,' Tommy said.

'I asked you all to be here, because I don't want to get stuck in anything again,' Aidan laughed, 'but also because I know that you are all really invested in this. I haven't gone in yet, I waited for you all. Maybe it's not there, but I really think it must be. It makes sense.'

'There's a top bit,' Aoife said, 'and a bottom bit. I think the limestone rocks went in at the top and the ash came out at the end. The council workers have done a lot of work around the top, but they haven't touched the bottom bit yet.'

'So, there's a good chance it's down there,' Billy said.

Aoife and Billy helped Aidan pull aside grass and briars and finally a small opening was revealed.

The others gathered excitedly around them.

'Let me have a look in there,' Aidan said. 'Aoife, will you shine the torch on it?'

He pushed his way through dirt and grass and finally got his head inside the opening and was able to kneel. Slowly he shone the torch around him.

'What do you see? Aoife asked excitedly.

'Stone walls and a lot of spider webs,' Aidan replied.

'Ugh,' Darragh shuddered. 'I hate spiders.'

Aidan felt the walls around him gingerly, wondering would there be a loose rock. He pushed several but nothing happened.

Ten minutes later, having felt every rock and crevice, he climbed back out, dejected.

'Wrong again,' he said sadly.

'Hang on,' John said, 'look at your knees, they are soaking. What's the soil like?'

'Wet and boggy,' Aidan said.

'Like all the soil around here,' Tommy laughed.

'What if it's not hidden behind a stone?' John asked. 'What if he buried it? Doesn't boggy soil preserve things?'

Aidan scrambled to his feet and was back next to the kiln in seconds.

Hurriedly, he dug with his fingers, the soil moving easily. The space was cramped, and his knees were almost blocking his way. He had to keep moving and digging.

'Anything?' Aoife shouted again.

'Not yet,' Aidan shouted back.

But then he felt it, something cold, something hard.

Oh my God, he thought.

Then fear went through him. What if it wasn't

the Lost Cup, what if it was a skeleton? Aidan felt like jumping right out of the kiln. What if it *was* the Lost Cup? Would it be bad luck to find it? But still his fingers moved, scraping, pulling.

Yes, it did feel like metal. Finally, in the faint light from the torch where he had angled it, he could see silver.

'I think it's here!' he roared.

'Well stop the lights,' he heard Tommy shout excitedly. 'Have Twin Power finally gotten something right?'

Aidan ignored him and kept working, digging, pulling. His nails were stinging, his arms were sore, but he kept going.

After what felt like an eternity, Aidan emerged sweaty and dirty from the opening in the kiln but holding aloft ... the Lost Cup!

Aoife ran to her brother and hugged him tightly and before he knew it, they all descended on him, his five friends from Droichead and the four from Gorman and they had lifted him up, up in the air and he was being carried, like John Power surely was when Coyle Gaels won the Cup all those years ago.

Carried by Droichead and Gorman players too, the same as his ancestors.

After several laps of the clearing holding Aidan and the Cup aloft, they finally collapsed in a heap on the grass in front of the kiln and sat, tired but elated in a circle with the Lost Cup in the middle.

'I can't believe it!' Aidan said, for about the hundredth time. 'I just can't believe it!'

'You've said,' Aoife laughed.

They examined the cup, and there it was, the last inscription: was Coyle Gaels winners 1922, captain John Power.

'Wow,' Billy said.

'Look,' Tommy said suddenly, 'look at the year before. Coyle Gaels winners 1921, captain Thomas Doyle. That must be my great-great-grandfather. He must have been the captain the year before John Power.'

'He was a good man according to my Grandad Joe,' Aidan said solemnly. 'He tried to keep the peace between Droichead and Gorman men during the Civil War.'

'Not like me,' Tommy laughed sadly.

'We've all had stupid moments fighting with each other, Tommy,' Aidan said seriously. 'Aren't we all getting on much better, thanks to you helping me out of the well?'

'I suppose,' Tommy nodded.

'I keep thinking,' Aidan said, 'of the horrible things that happened between Droichead and Gorman people, our own ancestors, a hundred years ago, during the Civil War. Billy's great-great-grandfather lost his leg from a gunshot, and our great-great-grandfathers, Thomas Doyle and John Power, tried to fix things. John Power's way of doing this was by hiding the Lost Cup.'

'What does it mean now that you have found it?' Sara asked.

'I don't know,' Aidan admitted. 'I hope it's a good thing. Maybe people will learn more about the Civil War, and make sure we don't turn against our neighbours again.'

'I think it's a good thing,' Aoife reassured him. 'It feels like a good thing.'

'The history book said the Cup was divisive, meaning it split people up, but I think we have changed that now. This Cup has brought us all together, Gorman and Droichead,' Aidan said.

Everyone nodded.

The chatting and 'I don't believe its' continued for a long time, as the ten kids sat in a circle. They were still there an hour later, when Mr Power, on a walk with his mother and father, Joe and Mary, gaped in amazement at the sight of the Lost Cup, a hundred years hidden, in the middle of a gang of Droichead and Gorman kids.

CHAPTER 21

'**A**re you ready, Aidan?' Aoife asked her brother.

'Yup,' Aidan grinned, walking out of his bedroom in a slightly-too-large Coyle Gaels jersey over a tracksuit and runners.

Aoife grinned back at him, wearing a matching jersey with the same tracksuit and runners.

'Twin fashion,' their mam laughed from the end of the stairs as the twins started to walk down towards her.

'We've never worn Coyle Gaels jerseys before,' Aidan smiled.

'Ah, Grandad, don't cry,' Aoife said, noticing her

180

Grandad Joe, who was standing next to her mother and father at the end of the stairs.

'Nana, not you too,' Aidan smiled as Mary sniffed loudly into a tissue.

'I'm sorry,' their grandad said, 'I'm just so proud of you both. Finding the Lost Cup, settling your differences with the Gorman kids, and now seeing you in the Coyle Gaels jersey. It's an honour to wear that, you know. To be picked as one of the best from Droichead.'

'We're only wearing it for a photo shoot!' Aoife laughed.

'Not just any old photo shoot,' Mary scolded them. 'A TV report as well! National press, local press, TV cameras, the whole lot, imagine at our lime kiln and reporting on our grandchildren and their friends.'

She dissolved into fit of tears again as Grandad Joe hugged her.

'C'mon, let's get going,' Mr Power urged them, 'the TV crews won't be happy if we're late!'

The Powers set off as a group from Amber Fields. It was a Saturday morning in September and the sun was still hot. They headed through the village and towards the bridge. Hordes of cars, trucks and outside broadcast vehicles lined the one small street through Droichead and bunting in the colours of Droichead Beag GAA, red and black, hung from every building.

The Powers walked down below the bridge, onto the Greenway and walked quickly towards the clearing where the lime kiln was. Clare ran excitedly ahead, and Mrs Power cautioned her several times to slow down and be careful of the river.

Arriving at the clearing, the twins couldn't believe their eyes. A huge crowd thronged the area. More Droichead black and red bunting was strung up everywhere. Everyone seemed to be waving either a Droichead flag or a blue and white Gorman flag. Garda Cleary was there and several volunteers in high-vis vests were directing people where to sit and stand. Several rows of chairs had been set up near the picnic tables, facing the lime kiln and they were all full, except for an empty row at the top, which was, to Aoife and Aidan's amazement, reserved for them, the Power family.

Big cheers rang out as the Powers took their seats. Aoife and Aidan turned and grinned at their friends sitting behind them. Billy, the Donovans, Tommy, and the Doyles were in the row directly behind them. Behind them again were Tina and the O'Sheas, Sara and the Novaks, then John, Darragh, Maeve, Ellie and their families. Billy gave Aoife and Aidan a reassuring squeeze on the shoulder and the twins settled down and took a deep breath.

Matt Kelly, the historian who had taught the twins so much about the lime kiln, and well-known TV presenter Daniel Horan were standing in front of the crowd, close to the lime kiln. The Lost Cup as it was now known across the country was sitting proudly on a podium. Four ribbons were hanging off it, one was red and black for Droichead, one was blue and white for Gorman, one was black and white to represent Coyle Gaels and the final one was the green, white and gold of the Irish flag. Next to it on a table, was Aoife's painting of the lime kiln in a beautiful oak frame.

'Can I have your attention please, ladies and gentlemen, boys and girls,' Daniel Horan began. 'I am delighted to welcome you all here today to Droichead Beag. Very shortly, we are going to talk to the man of the hour, Aidan Power, about his amazing discovery. First, I would like to call on the Minister for Rural Affairs and Heritage, Mary Devlin to say a few words.'

'Wow,' Aoife mouthed to Aidan. 'Someone from the government is here.'

Aidan stared open mouthed.

'I can't believe this is all because of us,' he hissed to Aoife.

'Because of you,' Aoife grinned at her brother.

'*A cháirde go leir,*' the minister started speaking. 'Welcome to you all on this beautiful September day. I am in awe of the work that has been done here in Droichead Beag in creating this beautiful river walk and in the stunning restoration of the lime kiln behind me. Let me just say how unbelievably impressed I am at the tenacity and perseverance of young Aidan Power in his quest to find the Lost Cup. He has done us a huge service in uncovering a piece of our Irish history that we thought lost for so long.

'This Cup is so much more than just a cup, signifying as it does the importance of our Gaelic games, which survived both the War of Independence and the Civil War and are more popular than ever today. In the hiding of this cup, it also signifies the lengths that one brave man, John Power, went to in trying to restore peace amongst neighbours who were torn apart and put in impossible positions during the Civil War. They were worn down from years of bloodshed, and how lucky we are to have peace on our island today.'

A loud clap went up from the crowd. Aidan noticed that his nana and grandad were crying again.

'It is also incumbent on us to remember men like William Donovan, who was injured during these times and Thomas Doyle, another peacemaker. So today, let us remember our ancestors, let us thank them for the sacrifices that they made. Let us commend Aidan Power and his group of friends, from both here in Droichead and in Gorman I am told, who combined to recover this lost treasure.'

A huge cheer went up from the crowd.

'After today's festivities,' Minister Devlin continued, 'the Cup will be taken to the GAA Museum in Croke Park, where it and its story will be on show for ever more for everyone to see. Thank you for your warm welcome and enjoy the rest of the day.'

A polite clap followed and Daniel Horan, the TV presenter stood up again.

'I can't believe Daniel Horan is here,' Tina whispered to Sara.

'I know, he's so handsome,' Sara replied dreamily.

'Give it a rest, girls,' John said rolling his eyes, 'look, Aidan is starting to talk.'

'Erm, thanks very much, Daniel,' Aidan was saying shyly. 'I suppose I started looking for the Lost Cup because it sounded cool and mysterious. Also, I was having a tough time at football, not playing great, so it was something to distract me.'

'From what I hear, you don't ever have a bad day at football, Aidan,' Daniel laughed, 'I hear that yourself and your sister are Powers through and through, footballing geniuses.'

'Ah, we have off days too,' Aidan laughed. 'I definitely had a few this year for sure. Aoife didn't.'

Aoife went bright red in the front row.

'Football genius,' Billy mocked her good-naturedly from the row behind, taking off Daniel Horan's accent.

'I hear that you fell down a well in the search, is that right,' Daniel kept going.

'Yeah,' Aidan laughed. 'That wasn't supposed to happen. I was a bit obsessed with finding the Cup at that stage. I have Tommy Doyle to thank for pulling me out of that situation, literally.'

Aidan was finding his flow now and the crowd were laughing along at the telling of the story. Annie Doyle smiled fondly at her son Tommy at this part.

'Tell me how you realised the Cup was in the lime kiln,' Daniel asked.

Aidan recounted the story of seeing Aoife's' painting and the photos and the crowd 'oohed' and 'aahed' at the painting.

'But how were you sure?' Daniel persisted.

'I don't know,' Aidan answered truthfully, 'I just knew.'

'And Aoife agreed with you?' Daniel asked.

'When I said I knew it was there, she just knew too,' Aidan said quietly. 'It's a twin thing.'

'Isn't that lovely?' Daniel smiled and the crowed 'aahed' again.

'This is an amazing story and well done again,

Aidan,' Daniel said. 'Now, I believe Joe Power, grandson of John Power and grandfather of Aoife and Aidan, would like to say a few words. The lime kiln is on Joe's land and belonged to the Power family when it was in use.'

Joe walked slowly to the podium and began to speak.

'I won't keep you long, folks,' he said. 'I wanted to say that when my grandson Aidan kept asking me about the Lost Cup, I refused to talk about it. I thought that no good would ever come from that Cup seeing the light of day again. I knew what had happened to William Donovan, and I thought it was cursed.

'I should have known that being a Power, Aidan wouldn't take no for an answer. I should have been honest with him and Aoife from the start and explained the situation properly. Our young people need to learn about our history, to make sure that nothing like that happens again and so that they learn the value of peace. It should be noted also that John Power went on to help bridge the divide between pro- and anti-treaty supporters after the truce. Coyle

Gaels had fallen apart during the later stage of the Civil War, but John Power and Thomas Doyle were instrumental in getting it going again, getting the men playing together and starting to heal Civil War wounds.

'In fact, in the finding of the cup, Aidan has brought about a different kind of peace. Peace for himself, because he set himself a mission and he succeeded, even if he caused a bit of bother along the way, getting stuck in wells and the like.'

The crowd laughed and Aidan blushed.

'But he also managed to unite his own gang of friends and a Gorman group of friends, who were, from what I hear, sworn enemies last summer. Aidan, I think that in the finding of the Lost Cup, you have brought about your own kind of peace, in the vein of John Power, albeit in very different times.

'Three cheers for my grandchildren, Aoife and Aidan Power, and their friends, Billy, Tina, Sara, John, Darragh, Tommy, Ellie and Maeve.'

'Hip, hip hooray!'

The crowd cheered.

'Before I finish,' Joe said, 'I want to remind you

about the rest of the day's festivities. This evening, we will have dinner and dancing in the marquee next to Kathleen's café, all are welcome.

'Before that, we are all headed to Carrick for the under-12 championship final between Droichead and Gorman. So, all the peace that Aidan has created will be forgotten for sixty minutes on the pitch.'

A big laugh went out again from the gathered Gorman and Droichead crowd.

'A special mention for my granddaughter, Aoife, her friends Tina and Sara and all her fellow female players on the team. It's their last match for Droichead Beag GAA, but I know that they will have a long and happy career playing for our new club Droichead/Gorman ladies' football club. Droichead Beag GAA will miss you, girls.'

Another big cheer rang out and Joe walked back to his seat to rapturous rounds of applause.

With the ceremony complete shortly afterwards, the large crowd began to disperse.

The Gorman and Droichead kids looked at each other warily.

'Time to get ready for this final,' Billy said breaking the silence.

'See you later,' Tommy winked.

CHAPTER 22

Aoife, Aidan, Billy, Tina, Sara and John sat outside the changing rooms in Carrick. It was 2.30pm. Throw in was at 3pm. Inside the changing room, various members of the team busied themselves with getting ready.

'Team talk in ten minutes,' Mr Power said, walking past them.

'OK, Dad,' Aoife and Aidan chimed.

'So, this is it,' Billy said solemnly

'Our last match playing with you boys,' Aoife said.

'I feel very emotional,' Sara sniffed.

'I know, right?' Tina agreed. 'I mean, it's not like we're moving away, we'll still see each other all the time, but it's just weird.'

'I wish they could change the rules,' Aoife sighed.

'Well, life changes, Aoife, unfortunately,' John said seriously.

'OK, old man,' Aidan laughed slapping John on the back good-naturedly. 'But you know, there are Féile competitions next year at under 14. That's something to look forward to.'

'What's Féile?' Sara asked.

'It's a big competition, where under-14 clubs from all over the country compete against each other. We'd get to go on a bus and stay overnight and play loads of other clubs,' Aidan replied enthusiastically.

'That's just you boys,' Sara sighed.

'There is a girls' under-14 Féile too,' Aoife said excitedly. 'I'd forgotten about that, that *is* something to look forward to!'

'Also, I heard a rumour that Droichead GAA are setting up a hurling team,' Aidan said.

'What, sure we wouldn't know what to do with a hurley,' Billy laughed.

'We could learn,' Aoife said. 'If those women in the 1900s could play it in that gear, I'm sure we could give it a go!'

'Right, let's focus now gang,' Aidan said, 'forget about it being the last game for the girls, forget all that, we need to beat Gorman. They beat us in the league, now it's our turn.'

'Yeah, we don't want to feel disappointment like the league final again,' Billy added.

'Absolutely not,' John agreed. 'I certainly don't want a broken ankle again.'

'Lads, it will be our finest hour, I can promise you that, won't it, Tina, Sara?' Aoife said passionately. 'Our last match for Droichead Beag GAA is going to be one to remember.'

'C'mon, Droichead, Droichead!' Aoife broke into a chant.

And so it was that when Mr Power arrived for his team talk a few minutes later, he didn't have much to say at all, as he was faced with his entire team, full of positive, enthusiastic energy, jumping around and chanting their team's name.

I have a good feeling! he thought to himself smiling.

At 3pm, the teams took their positions on the pitch. Aidan and Billy took up their usual spots in midfield for the throw-in.

'Who's that walking towards us with Darragh?' Billy asked Aidan, at the sight of two tall figures walking toward them, their opposite numbers from Gorman.

'Is it Tommy?' Aidan asked incredulously. 'He doesn't play midfield.'

'It is,' Billy laughed. 'I didn't expect that.'

'Well, boys,' Tommy smiled as he approached them. 'We're full of surprises in Gorman. I fancied a bit of a midfield battle today with my two favourite Droichead boys.'

'Bring it on, Tommy,' Aidan smiled in return.

'Ready boys,' the referee said. 'NO funny business.'

'No, sir,' Tommy said seriously.

'May the best team win,' Billy said as the referee threw the ball in the air.

'That team is Gorman!' Darragh shouted at the very same time as Aidan roared, 'That team is Droichead!'

The crowd in the stand watched as Aidan leapt higher than ever before, over the heads of Billy, Darragh and Tommy, grabbed the ball and took off running, sunlight gleaming on his black and red jersey of Droichead Beag GAA, Darragh and Tommy right on his tail.

Twins, Aoife and Aidan Power, are amazing Gaelic footballers. They and their four best friends love GAA! But are local rivalries getting out of hand as the children of Droichead Beag National School fight tooth and nail to make sure they – and not their rivals, Gorman – get their hands on the coveted Star Schools Cup.

READ MORE GREAT SPORTS BOOKS FROM THE O'BRIEN PRESS

Winner of four All-Irelands, 11 All-Stars and five Club All-Irelands.

When Cora was young, she was small for her age, and had to prove herself at every level: to the boys in her club, to the Mayo selectors who took a chance on her as a teenager, but most importantly to herself. From Croke Park to the stadiums of Sydney, Cora has proved herself to be a master of the game.

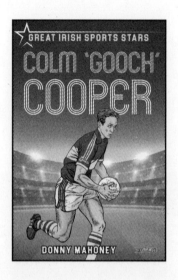

GREAT IRISH SPORTS STARS

COLM 'GOOCH'
COOPER

DONNY MAHONEY

The Gaelic footballer who's won
nearly every prize in the game:
Including 5 All-Irelands & 8 All-Stars

How a boy who everyone said wasn't
big enough or strong enough to wear
the green and gold jersey of Kerry
became one of the greatest Gaelic
footballers of all time.

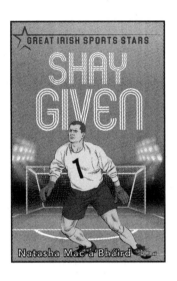

From the time he was a young boy playing with his brothers in
Donegal, Shay Given dreamed of football glory. He left home at
just sixteen to join Celtic and worked hard to become a world-class
goalkeeper. It paid off – the boy from Donegal went on to play for
top clubs like Newcastle United and Manchester City, played in the
Champions League, and made some amazing saves for Ireland at the
World Cup and the European Championships.

The inspirational life story of the Republic of Ireland's longest-
serving player.

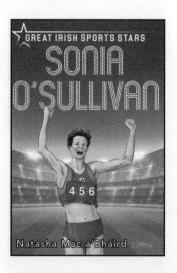

As a little girl, playing with her friends in Cobh, Co.
Cork, Sonia O'Sullivan was known as the fastest runner.
When she joined a running club and started to win
races, she began to dream of the Olympic Games.
Through her talent, dedication and her ability to get
back up and dust herself down when things went
wrong. Sonia went from an ordinary girl who loved to
run to an extraordinary world class athlete.

The story of one of Ireland's greatest ever athletes --
and a dream made real.

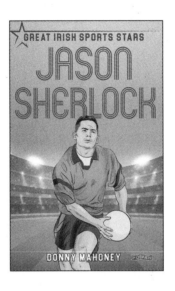

GREAT IRISH SPORTS STARS

JASON SHERLOCK

DONNY MAHONEY

Jason Sherlock loved every sport going; he played
basketball and soccer for Ireland and hurled with a
Cork GAA club. But he found his true calling in
Gaelic football and went all the way to the All-Ireland
final with the Boys in Blue. After his inspiring playing
career, Jason would go on to become a trusted assistant
for Jim Gavin during Dublin's historic five-in-a-row
run.

Discover how a boy from Dublin found strength in his
difference to become a Gaelic football great.

Growing up with

tots to teens and in between

Why CHILDREN love O'Brien:

Over 350 books for all ages, including
picture books, humour, fiction, true stories,
nature and more

Why TEACHERS love O'Brien:

Hundreds of activities and teaching guides,
created by teachers for teachers,
all FREE to download from obrien.ie

Visit, explore, buy
obrien.ie